By Same Author

Novels

The Death Certificate
The Lady with A Beard
The Lady with the Sting
The Day God Blinked
The Bad Samaritan
What A Next of Kin
Exhumed, Tried and Hanged
She Seized the Balls
Patching A Broken Dream

I0562020

Poetry

Crying in Hiccoughs

Alobwed'Epie

UNTIL

I

SINNED

Miraclaire Publishing
Kansas City (MO)/Yaounde

MIRACLAIRE PUBLISHING LLC
Kansas City, (MO) USA

Website: *www.miraclairepublishing.com*
Email: *info@miraclairepublishing.com*

P.O. Box 8616
Yaounde, Cameroon

ISBN-13: 978-0615957678
ISBN-10: 0615957676

Printed in the United States of America

Miraclaire Publishing makes every effort to ensure the accuracy of all the information ("Content") in its publications. However, Miraclaire and its agents and licensors make no representations or warranties whatsoever as to the accuracy, completeness, or suitability for any purpose of the Content and disclaim all such representations and warranties, whether expressed or implied to the maximum extent permitted by law. Any views expressed in this publication are the views of the author and are not necessarily the views of Miraclaire.

Chapter One

I cannot say with certainty what my childhood life was like. I can only say from a recast of childhood memories that I was born and bred by two stonewalls – my father and my mother. I cannot remember ever seeing them speak to each other, not to talk of seeing them exchange gifts. I believe they communicated instinctively, the way animals do to decipher the intensions of one another and react accordingly. I say this because in spite of that aloofness, there seemed to be an indescribable or telepathic system that made my mother know exactly what my father needed at any given time. She would call me and say, go and give your father this or that – mostly kitchen products of food and water which to me did not constitute gifts. I cannot remember ever hearing them laugh or cry together or singly. All I can remember is that they promptly went to congratulate beneficiaries of good fortunes or sympathize with victims of misfortunes, but kept mute while other sympathizers expressed their concerns. Nothing tended to be important beyond their physical presence in an event.

Our compound was perched on the third and more habitable step of the rocky Mendankwe eastern precipice overhanging Bamenda Township. The step is about sixteen metres wide where my father's main building stood, and about eight metres wide on both sides of the building where our mothers' three huts stood. The whole environment looked like an abandoned quarry with boulders overhanging precariously from cliffs and peaks behind the buildings. The compound was strewn with rocks, probably the products of centuries of rock avalanches washed clean of mud by torrential rains. My father had used some of the rocks in building the houses and a thick wall in front of the compound to prevent human beings, livestock and household things from slipping and rolling down the precipice. It may be the abundance of building materials attracted him to the place and he used them without reserve.

The walls of the buildings were about half a metre thick with pigeonhole-like windows overhung by the drooping eaves of the thatched roofs. This made the interiors of the buildings permanently dark even in the sunniest day. My mother's hut was built on the shorter and more spacious northeastern flank and her two co-wives' huts on the longer northwestern flank. I believe each hut occupied less than a hundred square metres of land. With that little space each wife exhibited her ingenuity in land management. Each dug out protruding rocks that impaired movement and piled them on the wall and with that the wall grew in size and length. In case of potholes, each filled them with stones to obtain a convenient compound for easy hopping from the huts to the main house, and finally each provided space for fowl and goat pens.

Although two springs cascaded a few metres north of the compound, we could only hear them gushing and lapping in inaccessible canyons. The approach to the compound was steep, very steep; almost vertical if one took the shortcut to the main road where the springs were accessible. That was the path we took to go and fetch water every morning at the five o'clock   first toll of the cathedral bell. The cathedral was one step below our step and if its bell tolled, the vibration resonated under our beds with the effect of a mysterious hand shaking us out of bed. With that, we the children yawned, got up, stretched ourselves and with chattering teeth and running noses 'cascaded' in the manner of the springs down the precipice to the main road where the springs emptied their waters in a gutter. We then filled our water containers and took the longer but gentler path to the compound. By the second toll at six o'clock we had made three such runs. I for one was expected to fill the three big water containers placed by the eaves of my mother's hut.

Brought up in such circumstances, I might have become a stonewall myself. I cannot remember having laughed or cried or complained in carrying out the household chores I did with the nimbleness of a machine. I am the lone child of my mother. I can't say with certainty what that meant to her. She never praised me even if she met the water containers full. She never scolded me if they were empty. But something tended to tell me that she was grossly hurt whenever she found the containers partly empty. So, I preferred to fill them and speculate on her internal favourable reaction. I did that with other household problems and that became routine. It is difficult to discuss my father. I hardly saw him. I rather heard him from a distance. He left the compound before we got up or when we had gone to fetch water and returned late in the evenings after we had put his food in his house and retired to our respective huts. He announced his return by singing in half-breath climbing the steep path. What he did for a living I never knew. My mother and her two co-wives did not seem to care much about where he went and when he returned. They were however punctual with his food and water.

I cannot remember that I once saw my father give his wives food money. Each of his wives had fowls and a few goats. They cultivated food crops and vegetables down the valley and sold them in the markets. Perhaps from the proceeds, they fed him and us. My mother's co-wives each had four children – two boys and two girls, and one boy and three girls respectively. The more children a wife had the more mouths she had to feed. So, each of us had to assist our mothers to provide the food and any other means of subsistence. As we grew up, we learnt to till the soil with them. We learnt to keep animals and we learnt to sell in the markets. Whatever we sold, we gave the money to our mothers. What they did with the money I did not know. But they bought us dresses at Christmas.

Though the toll of the cathedral bell was reminiscent of water-fetching, it pleased me perhaps because it reminded me of going to church on Sunday. I liked going to church because it gave me the opportunity to wear the dress my mother bought for me at Christmas. Once I changed my dress, I washed the workaday one which I wore from Monday to Saturday in rain or shine, in bed or awake. I had to wear it and wear it out for another to be bought next Christmas.

In church, I admired the Reverend Sisters. They were white and wore white from head to toe. They looked like angels. We were told angels were white. They had no children. We were told angels had no children. They sang beautifully. We were told angels sang beautifully. They spoke their language, the white man's language. We were told angels spoke the white man's language. They did not commit sin. We were told angels did not commit sin. I admired every aspect of the Reverend Sisters. One day, I saw a black Reverend Sister. She wore white from head to toe. She did everything like the white Reverend Sisters. But could she be an angel? Whether she could or not, in the fourth week of her being in the Mission, she assembled all the children for a brief meeting. She said she wanted to know whether we went to school or not and whether we were attending doctrine classes. Most children shied away from telling the truth but I put up my hand and said most of us did not go to school because our parents did not want us, mostly the girls, to go to school. With that she undertook a crusade to persuade parents to send their daughters to school. When she met my father, he said if our mothers were interested in sending us to school he would not object. Our mothers accepted and a new phase of our lives started.

Going to school entailed extra burden on our mothers. They had to pay school fee and buy uniforms and books for us. This of course meant that we had to increase our assistance in the pursuit of money. In addition to fetching water, tilling the soil and taking care of the animals, we fetched firewood after school each day and sold it in the market on Saturdays. Thus though our mothers posed as the main sponsors, we were self-supporting. In school, the Rev. Sisters showed remarkable affection for me. They always asked me to work in their house while other pupils worked in the school garden. I assisted them in baking bread and frying other pastries. They admired me in several ways – in the way I did the work of three or four kids put together without complaining, and in the way I comported myself and in the way I handled their utensils. Before long, I became very skillful in bread and cake baking. With that, the Rev. Sisters could supply all the Parish Priests with cake and bread. One day, the black Rev. Sister called me and told me that they had decided to exempt me from paying school fee. I jumped up excitedly in appreciation and when I got home and told my mother about it, I saw her for the first time exhale excitedly in appreciation also. By the time I was completing primary school, Our Lady of Lourdes College was opened and I was admitted in it.

My mother did not seem happy when I told her about my admission into the college. I suspected it could be because she feared she would be required to pay the fee. To dispel her fears, I told her my scholarship was extended to the college. In her characteristic manner, she kept mute, which to me meant approval. This was at the beginning of the three months holiday. I told her that I believed that I was given scholarship as a compensation for the work I did for the Sisters. I said it was therefore necessary for me to spend my holiday working with them. She kept mute, which to me meant approval. And so, I intensified my work with the Rev. Sisters. By the end of the holiday, they gave me money for uniforms and books.

My college life was unmarked. Our college was fenced and visits and outings were highly regulated. Since we were lodged and boarded and virtually permanently in school uniform, I had no need for dresses other than what I had. Even if visits and outings were more liberal, my parents were not the types that would visit. So I found it more convenient to go to the Rev. Sisters who readily showered me with praises and encouragement, than going to my parents. In the seventh anniversary of the founding of the college, the Rev. Sisters acquired a modern bakery and went into full commercial production of bread and pastries. They employed professional bakers and that diminished, so to speak, my role. In spite of that, they still welcomed me and provided me with essential human needs. I concentrated on my studies and in the end did the GCE Advanced Level and passed in three papers – Religion, English Language and English Literature with a compensatory in Geography.

I considered the results bad but they qualified me for entrance into a university. When I told my mother of my intension to go to the university, she sighed, which to me meant a categorical disapproval. This plunged me into self-reproaches. For the first time in my life, I felt the bile of hatred rise into my mouth. I blamed myself for telling a charlatan sponsor about my desire to further my education. My lips trembled as I fought against running her down. On second thought however, I decided to talk things over more amicably with her. She told me university education would require hundreds of thousands of francs in fee, lodging, feeding, equipment and movements. I lied that the Rev. Sisters had extended my scholarship and showed her the 75.000 Frs. they had given me to buy essential things. The money was actually the arrears of my stipend. With that, she shrugged her shoulders in approval, entered her room and brought out a purse from which she took 50,000 Frs. and gave me. Having won her battle, I knew that with my father was a foregone conclusion. And true to prediction, he did not only approve of my going, he gave me 30,000 Frs. with the promise that he would send more once he sold his cows. He said if he had known, he would not have bought so many cows. That was the day I knew he was a butcher. I can't express how I felt with that magnanimity. I had never had cause to begrudge my parents. I had all along taken them for what they were but that day; I thought I lived above the skies. A whole new world opened onto me. I had lovely parents. It was not very much the amount of money they gave but the fact that they gave and wished me well.

I had 155,000 Frs. to start with, and with my father's promise, I was confident I would make it to Yaounde. But I needed a person with whom to travel and be lodged for a day or two before I looked for my accommodation. Here I must confess, throughout my years at the college, I made no intimate friends. I saw and treated my classmates from a distance. Though I had no intimate friends, I had no enemies either. I knew Imelda my bench-mate had a brother in Yaounde. I took courage and approached her. I asked her when she would leave for Yaounde. She said in a few days. I told her I had never been to Yaounde and asked her whether she would be kind enough to allow me travel with her. She said there was no problem. I breathed in hard and asked her whether it was possible for her to inform her brother that she would come along with me and we'd stay with him till I got my accommodation. She scoffed deridingly. My heart quaked.

"I don't think he will accept. People in Yaounde don't like receiving more than one stranger because they lack space in their houses," she said.

"I shan't be long with him. Immediately we arrive, I shall look for my accommodation. I only need a place where I can spend the first and perhaps second night. Please," I supplicated.

"I shall inform him," she responded and I felt the air circulate around me.

Chapter Two

We left Bamenda on Thursday morning and arrived Yaounde in the evening. From every indication, Imelda's brother was ill prepared to receive us. His wife had travelled and it seemed she had prepared him food to last for some days before he could start worrying on what to eat. Immediately we entered the house, there was a gust of foul air to which we three reacted spontaneously by forcefully ejecting the stench from our nostrils with whistle-like noise. Our host immediately apologized. He said that a rat might have died at an unknown corner and promised to look for it in the morning. Although we were dead tired, I said we could not sleep in the house with such stench. I then opted to look for the dead rat by sweeping deep into dark corners. I swept out quite a sizeable chunk of dirt. In spite of that, the intermittent gusts of foul air continued. Accepting our defeat, we brought out the food we had brought from Bamenda and on trying to simmer it, we discovered the first source of the stench. The food his wife had left in the pots was in an advanced stage of decay. I got the pots and after empting the food in a pit, washed them very thoroughly. The stench abated. We simmered the food and ate some of it. What remained, Imelda took to the fridge. On opening the fridge a torrent of stench buffeted her face. She exclaimed and dashed back to the parlour. The food and meat in the fridge had terribly decomposed and that was the second source of the stench. Imelda developed nausea and started vomiting. I dashed forth, unplugged the fridge, took out the food and meat and threw them into the pit. Then I washed the fridge and left it open for some time before I put in the remaining food. As the air became more breathable our host told us his dilemma. He said he had warned his wife against preparing much food for him because he would be unable to simmer it and wash the plates after eating. Yet she prepared too much food to last for days. After having the first experience of washing plates, he abandoned the food in the pots and forgot about it. About the food and meat in the fridge, he said it got bad due to power failure. The house was miserable and he spent most of his time with friends. He said he was sorry for the inconveniences his negligence had caused us. Imelda had stopped vomiting. After chatting for a while, we went to bed.

I got up early the next day, washed the plates and swept the compound. When our host got up, he was surprised that I had done so much work while his sister was still sleeping. He partly thanked me and partly sympathized with me for having done so much work early in the morning. I told him I had to do it that early because I wanted to go looking for a house at Bonamoussadi.

"If you want a room at Bonamoussadi, then you have got one. My intimate friend is evicting some recalcitrant tenants from his six-room house. The unfortunate thing is that the house is by the road. Students don't like it because of the noise and insecurity. Two fellows have already advanced money for single rooms behind. The other two rooms and the commercial room and parlour are still unoccupied. I would have liked you and Imelda to school from here. You will not pay rents here. So, it's up to you," he said.

"When I see the place, I shall make up my mind. Bonamoussadi I hear is quite near the campus and so it would reduce transport cost," I responded.

"OK, if your friend gets up, we shall go," he said and moved away. Immediately he left, I became itchy to go and see the house. Imelda slept till 8.30. When she got up, it took her another hour to my dismay, to bathe and do makeup. We finally left for Bonamoussadi. I saw the house, studied the commerciality of the place and decided to take the room and parlour. It was 20.000 Frs. per month, payable in two installments. I pleaded with Imelda's brother to tell his friend to give me special concession by accepting payment in three installments. He agreed and I paid him 80,000 Frs. out of 145,000 Frs., I had left. The next day, I was in the comfort of my rented roof – unbelievably smooth.

But it was a big risk to spend more than half my capital on rents. Although my conciliation was that my father would send me money immediately he sold his cows, I hurriedly went and paid half my school fee and had only 20,000 Frs. left. That was not a bad figure to me. I hardly spent money. So I could manage with it till my father sent me the money. Three weeks into my stay at Bonamoussadi, I heard that one Mr. Njong, my father's friend had come from Bamenda. I rushed to see him. After the customary greeting cordialities, I asked him whether he saw my father before he came to Yaounde. He cast an ominous stare at me, breathed in hard and said, "I am sorry to tell you that he was arrested and charged with buying stolen cows. All attempts to bail him have failed. He is remanded in custody. The case may come up at any time."

I cast a blank stare at the speaker as a mysterious upward suction overwhelmed me and made my bowels move upwards blocking my chest. I felt as if I was losing balance. To protect myself from falling, I pinned my feet firmly on the ground. A billion stars circled in my eyes. After some time, I began regaining normalcy. Mr. Njong realized my state of shock and consoled, "Don't bother. We shall take care of the situation when things become calmer."

I can't remember whether I bid him goodbye or not as I left him. He called me back and gave me 10,000 Frs. I thanked him and returned to brood over my father's misadventure. I reproached God for allowing my father get into the snare of buying cheap cows which turned out to be stolen cows at the time that I had begun getting the feel of a father. I reprimanded myself for being the cause. If I did not insist on going to university, he might not have fallen into that trap. But no! My father did not fall into the trap because of my education. He had always been at the periphery. This swing in opposing viewpoints made me develop headache. I lay down and slept. When I got up, I took my stand. I had to survive. God had given me a commercial house at little or no effort. I must make use of it.

I took 5,000 Frs. out of the 10,000 Frs. Mr. Njong gave me and went and bought groundnuts at Mukolo market. I fried them, tied them in 100 Frs. scaled-up bundles, put the bundles in a transparent bucket and put a piggy-bank by the side of the bucket in front of my house. Customers came, opened the bucket, took bundles and put in the corresponding number of coins into the piggy-bank. In two hours, the groundnuts were finished. I got the piggy-bank and counted the coins. I got 8,000 Frs. with two flattened beer covers probably put in by a thievery rascal. I then made a deliberate study of my strategy. I questioned myself why my groundnuts sold faster than those of my neighbours. I realized that my groundnuts were of the specie called *country granot*. They were better fried and therefore more attractive. They were put in a cleaner container. The bundles were larger. I also discovered that if one took a little risk in having confidence in people, she could reduce the cost of labour at several fronts. If I had given the groundnuts to a peddler, I would have paid her at least 500 Frs. If I were seated at the door to sell to each customer, I would have either been tired or tempted to do charity with the groundnuts. I further realized that if I made 3,000 Frs. gain in two hours because I made bigger bundles, the turnover would be greater than if I made 5,000 Frs. gain with smaller bundles in a day or two, as my neighbours did. They grumbled at what they called blackmail and predicted that market trends would sooner or later; force me to reduce the sizes of my bundles. They did not understand the logic of fast turnover and so watched with dismay how my groundnut-selling grew by leaps and bounds in spite of what they termed suicidal bundles. And so I braced myself for survival in Yaounde

Chapter Three

The period between the time I moved to Bonamoussadi and the time Mr. Njong came to Yaounde was pretty relaxed because classes had not started. Registration was going on and so those of us who had come early and registered were idle. I used the period to establish myself in church. I saw the Parish priest and introduced myself to him as an x-student of Our Lady of Lourdes College. I told him about my relationship with the Rev. Sisters, how I assisted them in several ways, my interests and how I could be of help in running the church. He said he needed devoted volunteers to carry out God's work and advised me to start by joining The Legion of Mary and the choir. Soon after joining the two, I realized there was a vacuum in leadership. Group members squabbled for positions and lost focus. Meetings were poorly attended. Resolutions were never respected. Church contributions and alms were disgracefully low. Youths were defecting to other denominations. The elderly were feeble with broken faith. St. Peter's rock was becoming shifting sand and the Parish priest was by all standards helpless. The Rev. Sisters in Bamenda had taught us that in a situation like that; one should not take the cane but should teach by examples.

Registration was drawing to a close and classes were starting timidly. I made a bird's eye-view of the task ahead of me. I had to combine my studies, groundnut-selling and church work. To give each the attention it deserved, I made a timetable. **Monday to Friday**: 4.00 to 6. 00 a.m. (Groundnut-frying) 6.00 to 7.30a.m. (morning prayers and preparation for classes) 7.30 a.m. (breakfast/off for classes) 8.00a.m. to 5.00p.m. (classes) 5.15p.m. (return from classes, lunch/dinner) 6.00 to 7.30p.m. (choir practice/ Youth movement/ Legion of Mary meetings) 7. 30 p.m. (return form church) 8. 00 to 11. 00 (prepare next day's meal, read) 11. 00 to 4. 00 (Sleep) **Saturday:** 6.00 to 11.00a.m. (cleaning house/laundry/market) 11.00 to 12.00 noon (cook) 12.00 to 2.30p.m. (visit and prayer sessions in hospitals) 2.30p.m. (return from hospitals) 3.00 to 6.30p.m. (church-cleaning, choir practice) **Sunday**: 7. 30 to 12. 00 noon (church service) 12. 30 to 1. 30 p.m. (launch) 2. 30 to 4. 30 p.m. (visit and prayer sessions in hospitals) 4.30 to 7.30p.m. (preparing food for Monday). 7.30 to 11.00p.m. (fry groundnuts) 11.00p.m. to 4.00a.m. (sleep). Within a week, the timetable was flowing in my bloodstream and I became a robot.

Time flies when one is extremely busy. I was extremely busy. I was not doing very badly in school. Agreed, I never made high grades but I never failed a test. The situation in church was improving timidly but steadily. Groundnut-selling brought in hard cash. At a certain point, I tried making plantain chips. They sold like hot cakes. I included them in the menu. When Imelda told me that most of the students had already left for Christmas holiday and that she would be leaving in two days, I could not imagine that we had already done three months in Yaounde. Though I had wanted to prepare the church for Christmas, the urge to see my distraught parents took precedence and in two days we left for Bamenda.

I did not know how to approach our compound. I had two options – start crying from a distance to manifest the stabbing sorrow in me for the calamity that had befallen my father, or enter the compound stealthily, then slam myself onto the ground in front of his house and start crying and so bring his wives out to join me in crying for my imprisoned dear father. I chose the second option. When I got to his house, I raised my hands to the high heavens, shouted and forgetting that the compound was stony, slammed myself on the stones and started crying. I got hurt in the process. The first person who came out was my father. He held me and raised me and asked why I was crying. He suspected I had failed my exams. He led me to his house and made me sit down. His wives soon joined him and with genuine concern, they all asked why I was crying. I told them I was crying because Mr. Njong had told me in Yaounde, that my father was arrested and remanded in custody without bail.

"Yes, I was actually arrested and refused bail. But when the case came up, my enemies were surprised that I was acquitted. You see, God has a way of defending the innocent. It was my fellow butchers who mounted the coup. They wanted me out of the slaps and so connived with herdsmen to trick me to buy the cows. The cows were not actually stolen. But anybody who heard that I bought a cow for 30,000 Frs. said that only stolen cows could cost that low. And so, the police came and arrested me, charged me of abetting theft and remanded me in custody without bail. The conspirators hastened up the case with the intention of giving me no time to assemble funds and hire a lawyer. By the grace of God however, I got a tough lawyer. He advised me not to plead guilty. He said I should say I bought cheap, but not stolen cows. The prosecutor said I should have suspected from the price and where the cows were sold that they were stolen. In his defence, my lawyer asked the herdsman, "*Magida* is it not true that ten of the cows you sold were sick?" The fool responded that only one was sick. My lawyer clung on that. He argued that all the cows were sick and the herdsman was asked to eliminate them to prevent the spread of the disease but instead of doing so, he defied instructions and decided to sell the cows at giveaway prices, and that was why they were that cheap. He said the cows did not carry badges to warn customers that they were stolen and so any innocent person would have bought them. With that the case turned against my enemies and I won. But now, I can't do butchering anymore. If I try, they can physically eliminate me. So, I am ruined. What other trade can I start doing now at this age?" my father asked with a sinking voice, sure proof that he was deeply hurt.

I lack words to describe that hilarious moment. Although my father said he was ruined, I preferred him ruined at home than in prison. So, I thanked God a million times and prayed that He should forgive me for deriding Him when Mr. Njong broke the news to me. Then I led my family in an open thanksgiving prayer and after that, limped in pains to my mother's hut to arrange my bed. In spite of the pain, I spent a marvelous short holiday with my parents. For the first time, my father stayed at home for his wives and children to have his feel. He in return manifested great joy in being with us. Time and again, he moved around to see how we fared. Our mothers reciprocated with equal concern. Their new found devotion to him was manifested in the way they roasted corn as if they were tele-guided by some planetary force that made them send us the children to give him. From different kitchens we arrived at the door of his house at the same time and scrambled to give him the corn. He usually took mine first, broke it and gave me the tip of it, and did the same with the corn of my half brothers and sisters. We could not refuse taking the corn though we had eaten or had some in our respective kitchens. It was wonderful to receive a gift of corn from our new found father. Time and again I recalled the proverb, 'Every disappointment is a blessing'. Our father's dilemma had become a blessing.

In spite of that cordiality, I cut short my holiday to return to Yaounde to prepare the church choir for the New Year Mass and to launch the Christian Youth Movement (CYM). I had taught two songs before I left for holiday. We rehearsed them thoroughly and had a marvelous performance in church on New Year Day. The Rev. Father called it a new awakening. And really, it was a new awakening. Immediately we launched the CYM and went on a crusade to bring back all the youths who had changed denomination, church attendance and its accompaniments improved. This led the Rev. Father to suggest that we call for the election of a new bureau to run the choir. I objected. I knew he wanted to replace the choirmaster with me. If that happened it could split what I was trying to unite behind the screen. The choirmaster appreciated my suggestion and started working relentlessly to improve his image. In the Legion of Mary there was a uniform crisis. Some women refused buying the new uniform because they thought the President was showy. I studied the situation and found out that the recalcitrant faction was made up of mostly the poor. So I told the President to make me the sales agent. And once I was made that, I took the risk and lent out the new uniform to those who hadn't raw cash and asked them to pay in four installments. That defused the situation and the church started speaking with one voice.

The CYM unconsciously propelled me into big business. With a membership of children mostly below 16, we had a financial crisis from the word go. We needed money to run the bureau, to give snacks after meetings and for logistics and other eventualities. We twice tried to raise funds through church donations. The congregation reacted with sighs and clucks. So I told the CYM to gird their loins and suggest ways by which we would get funds to run the movement. The children made candid suggestions – get manual labour jobs like cleaning compounds, clearing farms, washing clothes and so on. Those jobs, to me, were not good enough. So, an idea came to me. I went to Bamenda and bought the old bakery equipment the Rev. Sisters had discarded when they installed the modern bakery. In fact, though I say I bought, they gave it to me at giveaway price when I told them the challenges our CYM was facing, and how I wanted to solve the problems. Upon my return, I set up a mini-bakery. I named it **Bright Day Bakery (BDB)**. That earned for me the nickname, **Miss Bright.** We first went in for the production of *chingching,* doughnuts and lightweight cakes. With that, I employed an adult manageress and the CYM on these terms – any member who came to work received a stipend with a deduction or 20% which went to the CYM coffers. The fact that members found themselves bagging 80% of their proceeds, made the attendance constantly heavy and very productive. Furthermore, the fact that I fed the children with what they produced made them over zealous to work. This posed the problem of discipline. Some children started abandoning school work. We were obliged then to limit the work to Saturdays and insist that only those who did their assignments and passed were to be allowed to work. With that, the children adjusted themselves. They worked devotedly and production increased by leaps and bounds. To protect my 'industry', I made a logo for special binding and got a patent license.

Our products were in high demand. We could barely satisfy hawkers. Even some of the CYM children became hawkers. We received orders from several homes and supermarkets. People who had occasions made special orders. We soon specialized in wedding-cake production. To maintain standards and maximum production, I was constantly at the bakery. This of course had adverse consequences on my school work. I never failed a test but I never made good grades. Imelda was particularly unhappy with my lifestyle – from school to church, from church to bakery.

Chapter Four

I could hardly call my situation second nature. It was first nature – I had never known the difference between the two. I was born to work, I was working, I would keep working. Work meant nothing to me. It was part and parcel of me. Imelda and others thought I was exaggerating. Although they came to borrow money from me from time to time, they did not approve of my schedule. We were now in year three – the last year of the first cycle of university education. I couldn't remember whether throughout my three years in the university I had had a conversation with a man on any other topic but business. There were cases of rape reported here and there. There were cases of boys fighting in girls' houses and vice versa. There were gossips about love betrayals. To me, all that was the devil's work in idle hands. The devil had easy access in lazy idlers. One day, Imelda came to the bakery and was told that I had gone to church and would be back in a few minutes. For two long hours she waited. When I finally returned, she unleashed the stop-cork of anger and erupted.

"Emerencia," she called almost shouting. "Work and church have become your second nature. You never take a break to visit friends or rest. I have been here for two hours. What type of church do you go to? If you die now what will you tell God you came to do on earth? Do you think the body goes to heaven? No, it does not. Only the soul goes. The comfort of the body is here on earth and so it must be well fed, clad, perfumed and relaxed, but your body is not only poorly fed, clad, never perfumed but it's permanently under stress. I don't even know how you pass your exams. I have tried to find out if you commune with the lecturers. But which lecturer would leave flashy girls and follow a one-gown-day-and-night girl?" she asked with a frown.

"Sister Imelda, good evening," I greeted her calmly, took her hands and kissed them. "I am sorry but thankful that you persevered to wait for so long. But are you so angry that you forgot to address me sister? Extreme anger leads to sin and sin leads to hell. So please, don't get angry and lose your soul. Please, get up and embrace your sister," I entreated. She got up and after embracing me, she calmed down. I gave her our latest product – a light cake with very little cholesterol.

"That's it," she said with a smack and got the packaging. After reading the logo she exclaimed, "So you are the one I hear people calling Miss Bright? OK, Miss Bright, I have come to tell you that soon after our final exams, my elder sister would be wedding. I have recommended you to make her wedding cake. The lady that makes a wedding cake presents it to the invitees before the bride and groom cut it. There is a wedding on the Saturday following the end of our final exam. I am the assistant protocol officer. I shall want you to attend it and see how wedding cakes are presented to the attendees. It is a big lesson you'll have to learn. You have to memorize every aspect of it. I have come this early to make sure that you programme yourself before that day. I don't want to hear that church matters have interfered with the plan."

'OK, if that is what has brought you, be rest assured that I shall be there. My only worry now is…"

"I know your only worry," she snapped. "You don't have dresses. I have incorporated you into the wedding maids group. In fact you are a maid of honour. Tomorrow I shall bring a seamstress here to take your measurements for the maids' uniform. Even if I don't come with her, be at home at six o'clock. Don't dictate how she should sew the gowns. All you have to do is surrender your body to her and she will take the measurements as it pleases her, not as it pleases you because I know you don't know your body."

"So even if the gown is too short and too tight to expose the contours of my body I should accept?" I asked.

"Yes," she responded dictatorially with no qualms. "The dresses are for a purpose and must be sewn to accomplish the purpose," she added authoritatively and stood up to go. I got some doughnuts and a cake and gave her and she returned.

The next day the lady came and took two measurements – one that indicated that the gown would be loose and floppy and one that indicated that the gown would be tight and short. I thought there was a girl of my bulk for whom the second gown was meant, so I kept quiet. After taking the measurements, I gave her a light cake. On tasting it, she smacked several times and asked who made the cake. I said it was Miss Bright. "Who is Miss Bright?" she asked. "I am the one" I responded. "You make such wonderful cakes! Have you some for sale?" she asked. "Yes," I responded and gave her one. She paid for it and left.

Some days later I met Imelda and asked her how much I would pay for the dress. She said all she expected from me was to wear the dresses. That was all. She and her boyfriend had undertaken to dress the wedding maids as their contribution to the wedding of her boyfriend's friend's wedding. "But can't I help you to reduce the cost?" I asked. "No," she responded in her dictatorial manner and added, "If you want to help me, I shall be wedding him at Easter. At that time, you can exhibit your financial might."

Imelda's talk of financial might unnerved me. I was caught between being angry with her and blaming myself for the truth of her rebuke. I was making money, real money for three years, but not spending it. My working capital had risen to 5 million francs. I had a saving account of 4 million francs. Many friends owed me. What was I going to do with so much money? And of course more was coming in by the minutes. An idea came into my mind. I would go to Bamenda after the wedding and buy a plot for my father at Abakwa, but not tell him until I built and asked them to move from the precarious step.

As our final exams got nearer, I never saw Imelda again. I suspected she was reading herself to death. I also read hard and when we sat the exam I was confident I would make it. With that, I was relaxed and looked forward to the day of the wedding. Although nothing tended to worry me, I believe Imelda thought I had very fuzzy knowledge of weddings and needed to be properly schooled. A few days before the D-day, she invited us the maids, to rehearse several aspects of the wedding – handling the bride's gown, throwing flowers at the couple, reading the Epistles and prayers in church, singing bride songs and other things. After the rehearsals the seamstress made us try on the dresses. Each bride maid had two – the floppy one that reached the ankles and had a belt for adjustment at the waist, and the very tight one at the waist with loosely pleated lower reaches that flew open with a little puff of the wind or whirl and exposed one's upper thighs and even the buttocks.

Both dresses fell short of my taste because minus the dreadful shortness of the short one, the necks had a broad u-shape that extended right to the shoulders thus exposing most of one's bosom and back. They were to be worn with strapless elastic bra that squeezed the breasts and made them bulge upward. In fact, I lost a heartbeat when I saw the middle portion of my breasts bulge out as if they had a quarrel with the bra. They looked like over ripe abscesses. I giggled at the damned thing and thought of telling Imelda that I won't wear the dresses. The seamstress was however ecstatic about her achievements. When Imelda saw us in the dresses, she was so thrilled that she jumped at me and exulted, "Lady Bright, you look really bright, cute and fantastic! Do you see what you have been depriving the world? What a majestic look! Please give her the big mirror. Yes, Miss Bri, there you are – supper sweet."

I shuddered from shame at the thought of being considered majestic in what to me was ostentatious and awfully immoral dressing. Before I had time to react, she was giving us instructions on how to move and squat when wearing either of the dresses. "When you wear the short one, you do not bend down to pick something from the ground. You squat, like this," she demonstrated. I pouted, eyed her rather scornfully and shrugged my shoulders.

Chapter Five

The dresses had made me lose interest in the wedding. But the English saying, 'One good turn deserves another' stuck in my neck and held me captive. Whatever I was becoming in Yaounde, I owed it to Imelda. And as the saying goes, 'If your friend braves the storm for you, you should brave dew for her.' Through her, I met her brother. Through him, I got the house I had converted into a money factory. Now she was asking me to reciprocate with learning how to present wedding cakes to invitees, so as to do the same in the wedding of her elder sister. Although that was a direct challenge to my piety, I thought I could temporarily step out of my 'cage' for her sake. And so, a day before the wedding day we went through a punishing exercise of hairdo. Throughout my life I had worn my hair low for easy maintenance. Now Imelda wanted hair transplant, some sort of ponytail that would overflow and sweep the bare back. She invited two of our colleagues who made a living out of hairdressing to carry out the job. For three hours they worked on my hair. By the time they finished, my neck cricked in excruciating pains. I complained. Imelda gave me some painkillers.

Next morning, the morning of the wedding, as early as six o'clock, Imelda came with a proficient makeup lady. The lady studied me methodically, made me sit on a chair inclined backward at 130 degrees and went in for the attack. She clucked, encased my hair in a plastic bag, and made me lean backward; and dipping a face towel in warm water, thoroughly massaged my face, chest and back. Then she applied a foamy substance on the face, chest and back (parts that were to be exposed) and sponged them dexterously. She applied another thick foamy substance and allowed it to dry. After some time, she scratched it at the edges and obtained two openings. She took hold and skillfully peeled off what now looked like a sloughing skin. While pulling off the 'slough', I felt as if it was pricking off the minute hair on my face. She did the same with the chest and the back. She examined the 'slough', examined my face, got a pin-like instrument and prickled my face with it apparently removing stubborn hair and black spots. That done, she applied what I would call 'mortar' to fill the little crevices perhaps created by the treatment.

After obtaining what Imelda later described as exquisite smoothness of the parts, she applied oils, powder and some pallid hue to match. She then glued artificial eyelids onto my eyelids, applied a light foamy liquid on my finger/toe nails and scraped them clean. She allowed the nails to dry, then she glued artificial nails onto the nails, trimmed and filed them to shape and applied purple nail polish. Then she sprinkled multi-coloured microscopic shining flakes onto my face, chest and back. They stuck and as they sparkled on my body, Imelda went wild with excitement. "Lady Bri, you will surely steal the show from the bride," she complimented.

The other bride maids did not receive much attention. Their makeup lasted a few minutes and very soon, at about 10 o'clock, we were off to church with the groom to wait for the bride. There was nothing spectacular in church worthy of our concern here, but for the fact that, for the first time in my life, I was in church not on deep meditation but on show-casing. I felt the vibrations of worldliness in my system. Air circulated around me as water in the gills of fish. We, the maids occupied the prime of place and that filled us with pride. I remember that at the time of consecration, I did not kneel down for fear of dirtying the floppy gown. I remember that when I went for communion I was not convinced I had prepared for it well. Mass ended at 4 o'clock having been started 2 hours late because of the late arrival of the bride. The reception which was scheduled for 5 p.m. started at 8p.m. Within that interval, Imelda decreed that the makeup lady should do a retouch. After it was done, she asked us to wear the short dress. I didn't mind it; after all, it was already night. But then, when we got to the banquet hall, it was as bright as day light. That astounded me and I almost melted in shame especially as I found myself at the high table where on sitting down, I exposed most of my thighs to curious eyes below. Imelda who was the assistant protocol personnel had made it in such a way that I sat where I would take note of all minute details concerning the introduction of wedding cakes to the invitees. She might have predicted my discomfort. To ensure that she kept me in place, she time and again came to whisper encouragement to me.

The MC read the programme, presented the President of the occasion and asked the Rev. Father to lead the invitees in prayer. Every other thing went according to plan. Then it came to the cutting of the cake. Imelda asked me to help the baker set it up. It was a three layered cake in the form of a pyramid. We carried it from the containers and set it on the table. Then the lady, a woman of no mean composure, dressed in a skirt shorter than mine, invited the couple for the cutting of the cake. The couple stood facing the audience – the cake in front of them and the lady by the side to give the audience a clear view of the cake.

"Michael and Susan," she addressed them. "I couldn't express my joy when I was chosen to make your wedding cake. In like manner, I can't express my joy in saying in making the cake; I chose colours that are so dear to me. If you look at the cake, you will see pink in the background of green and white. Pink is a divine colour, a colour of sublimity. Green is the colour of hope and fertility and white is the colour of peace. Be blessed as each of these colours would influence your stay together as husband and wife. Take hold of this knife then – Susan, hold first so that Michael can grip your hand with the knife and at the count of three, you should cut the cake. Oneeee. Twoooo. Threeeeee (applause)

Now, Susan you as wife and would be mother will now show us how you would feed Michael and the children. Cut the cake and feed him. (Wooooo, Applause) Michael, you as husband and would be father show us as you would fend and feed your family. Cut the cake and feed your wife. (Woooooo applause) Now embrace yourselves and go and sit down. (Wooooo applause)

The couple went and sat down. While all that was going on Imelda kept an eye on me and discovered that I was very attentive. Immediately the couple sat down she came and whispered, "As simple as that." It was now time for entertainment. She withdrew to organize the girls prepare the tables. I realized that there was disorder and sloppiness in the way the girls carried out the task. The ceremony had started late, people were eager to eat and dance. The girls were slow. For almost an hour the tables were not ready. When Imelda came to talk to me, I told her I wanted to organize the girls. "No', she decreed. "You are here to be served and not to serve. Sit down and have the honour to be served." Food and drinks were finally served and after entertainment the couple was asked to open the floor.

Immediately the couple opened the floor and returned to their seats, the MC invited the attendees to the floor. A thousand hands came to ask me for a dance. I picked one gentleman, I can't tell why. We danced in a God-fearing manner – keeping a good distance from each other and keeping mute as we danced. To be candid I was dancing in a formal place of dance for the first time in my life. I don't know whether I danced well or not. All that was necessary was to stand up and shake the body. Had dance a deeper meaning? I didn't know. The record ended and we separated. A new one was put and a gentleman rushed to take me. After dancing with five gentlemen in the God-fearing style, a tall gentleman asked my hand in dance. Immediately I stood up, the lights were dimmed. The gentleman seized my hands and pulled me close, too close for my liking. He pinned his chest onto my bosom and fiddled with my buttocks. Then he started a conversation asking me how I felt, where I came from, when I came to Yaounde, where I lived and what I was doing for a living. He introduced himself as the Assistant Director of Camtel. I can't tell at that time whether we were dancing or conversing. Everything was a bunch of rubbish. I pushed him away, abandoned him on the dance floor and went and sat down in rage at a corner and never danced again. Stupid.

Chapter Six

Imelda might have sensed my absence at the dance floor. She mounted a frantic search for me and discovered me brooding at the corner.

"Sister Emerencia, what are you doing there? Why are you so upset and bleary?" she asked.

"I have a throbbing headache," I responded.

"A throbbing headache, so sudden? I saw you dance with a gentleman. Then you disappeared."

"He was dancing immorally and so I abandoned him on the dance floor," I responded.

"How do you distinguish moral from immoral dancing? Should I call the driver to take you home?" she asked with a trembling voice.

"Yes," I responded firmly. She dashed away and presently, the driver came and took me home. Immediately I reached home, I took my prayer book and prayed to my Lord and Savior to forgive me for sins committed that day. Early Sunday morning I went for confession and received the body and blood of my Lord piously. For four days I did not see Imelda. I knew she was boiling with rage against me. That was her business. I stood my grounds. On Friday, I went to school to see if they had begun publishing results. I met her. She pretended not to have seen me and was about to sneak away when I called and rushed to hold her. She turned and said, "Back to square one," and hit her foot on the ground several times. I responded, "Back to square two," without knowing what she meant by back to square one.

"Emerencia do you know how much that makeup cost me? So immediately you got to that your factory that night you undid it to return to your square one? Come on," she invited and started dragging me from the other students. I followed her and when we got to a place out of earshot of the students, she erupted, "Emerencia, if you were a child I would have 'ssssllaapped' you now well, well. Do you know that, that makeup cost me 20,000 Frs.? That makeup would have lasted for three weeks if not a month, with minor retouching. Now, you in your ignorance have destroyed it. Which other girl had the luck of dancing with so many infatuated men, like you in that hall? Let me be frank with you Emerencia, we borrow money from you. What do you think we do with the money? Do you think we use it for food and drinks? No. We use it to buy clothes and cosmetics for makeup. We do makeup to enhance our ego for the world of men to know that we are there. Those who are affianced solidify their positions. Those who are not affianced scuttle to be affianced. Any flower that does not open its petals is not visited by flying insects meant to pollinate it. It is visited by black crawling insects that lay their eggs in its buds and destroy it. You think makeup is sin. It is not sin. It is simply complementary – renovating God's work. Now tell me what happened that night."

"I danced with six gentlemen, I alone, for the first time in my life. With the first five, we danced in a Christian way – each of us keeping a clean distance from the other. Then came in the last fellow, mad fellow. He seized my hands, dragged me to himself, pinned his chest onto my bosom and started fondling my buttocks – making me develop e e e. I saw that as a violation of my piety and so abandoned him on the dance floor. Stupid."

"Waaa! Emerencia, you caught an elephant and let it go? What a shame! You let go your God given sweetie because he fondled what belonged to him? What did you want him to fondle, your hands? Emerencia, do you know a woman is the custodian of a beggar's purse? He had to fondle your bosom and buttocks because that is what makes you a woman – that is what he does not have, that is what you are keeping for him. You would have also looked for what you don't have in him and fondled it because he is keeping it for you. Tell me Emerencia, how else would a man have manifested the effect of your arousing him without fondling you? See, those five impotent cowards you approved of their dancing are inconsequential. You have missed the real man. You have, and I feel bad. But as the saying goes, 'If the first throw of the hook does not bring a catch, put a more juicy bait and throw the hook back into the water'.

"Imelda, what you are saying is perhaps true but how do you allow yourself to be fondled by a man you have met for the first time? That fellow is a brute. I hate him."

"Emerencia, what he did is a pacesetter. There is no question of hatred in the whole thing. The man did not mean you harm. He did not know you. Something attracted him in you and he wanted to use the dance opportunity to start a relationship with you. You would have played on his intelligence by saying that you were afraid, his wife would hurt you. If he were married he would have stammered and told a lie that his wife wouldn't know. And that would have warned you on how to deal with him. If he were not married he would have said he was not married. And that would have led to starting a relationship. See, I met my boyfriend in a Bali Old Boys Association meeting dance hall. He was completing his High School education when I was in year four at Lourdes. He fondled me in the way that fellow fondled you. I told him calmly that I did not approve of that because it was a manifestation of rascality. Since he did not want to be associated with rascality, he asked me for a date. I told him I was ready to give him a date on condition that he assured my safety. He said he would. I told him I would tell my father that I was visiting him. He said that was OK. The day I visited him, he behaved the gentleman and we gave ourselves six months of observation. After that, he visited me and told my father he would want to marry me. My father said on condition that he allowed me complete my studies. He accepted and here we are today, sure as daybreak to get married at Easter. Dance floors are not the dens of devils. Most respectful partners today found each other in dance halls."

"I accept but, you see, I still believe that God arranges marriages. I think one can find the best partner in church where there is respectability and piety."

"That is your thinking. I wish you luck. But see it this way, a woman's active live is very short. Education has worsened things. Any girl who goes through secondary, high school and university education without having the luck of being affianced is doomed to remain single or go below the scale. That is why you see unmarried women who complete university studies scramble to have a second chance at Ecole Normale. And if they fail getting a husband even at Ecole Normale, they gird their loins for the rough times ahead. Remember that there are more women looking for men to marry than men looking for women to marry. Furthermore, you should know that married women are more likely to go to heaven than unmarried women. Isn't it that the Bible is more centred on married women and widows than on single women? I believe your bakery and church preoccupations have made you insensitive to all that," she said and left in the most arrogant manner.

I took her eccentric departure for a spite and thought of breaking our cordial relationship. However as I moved away from where she had abandoned me, I gave her rebuff a second thought. I took it as a complementary action to her revelations and decided to ponder over them more carefully. First, she was down to earth and fluent; which showed that she had nursed the grievance for a long time and had the opportunity to vent it out. Second, all what she said was true. Although we addressed each other sister and we were bench-mates at Lourdes, we were neither related nor age mates. We simply agreed to address each other sister, when she took me to her brother's house upon our arrival in Yaounde. She was several years my junior but much more versed in worldly affairs than I was. The truth is bitter. Hers was very bitter. I had been out of touch with reality for a very long time; and now, I was being buffeted by the pangs of reality. Because my upbringing had stifled my emotional life, marriage lingered at the periphery. My dead impulses had to be resuscitated to make me accept that I was part of humanity and therefore an obligatory candidate for marriage. I had assisted many couples getting married in church. But I had never considered it as something worthy of my concern. But now, Imelda's revelations had set fire on me and I saw my dilemma. I must get married. To attract the boys, I must do makeup – wear the false coat of beauty and even tell lies. I must go to dance halls and allow brats to fondle me. The stakes were varied. Suppose I accepted the fondling and things didn't work out favourably, I would be condemned to bear the stigma of misadventure for the rest of my life. The modern husband ruled out piety. What a world! But then, prayers do move mountains. So, my best option was to intensify my church work and prayers with a focus more on marriage than on any other thing. With that, I sang this song as I moved homeward:

> All who believe in, our Lord Jesus Christ
> Will never die;
> All who believe in, our Lord Jesus Christ
> Will never die;
> For the Lord is with them, and only with them
> They'll never die;
> For the Lord lives in them, and only in them
> They'll never die;
> As the Lord lives in me, and only in me
> I'll never die;
> As the Lord lives in me, and only in me
> I'll never die.

After singing and cooing and humming the song several times, I developed a running nose with intermittent hiccoughs emanating from deep seated guilt and regret. I almost broke into tears when I entered my house. The manageress of the bakery asked what was wrong. I told her I had a headache and I needed rest. Before I entered the room, she handed the money of the day's sales to me. I did not count it but went straight to bed and lay down. From there, I told her to close for the day. After they had gone, I got up and prayed that, the God I served should open the way for me. Let my husband come from pious surroundings – the church. Let me be blessed with children even at an advanced age; after all, Sarah begot at an advanced age. In spite of the prayer, I felt bad. My faith was shaken. But why? I did not know. So, I modified the wording of one of my favourite songs and sang it over and over again:

> Because Christ lives, I can face tomorrow,
> Because He lives, my fears are gone,
> I know oo, He holds my future,
> And my life is worth living because He lives.
> Because He lives, I can face tomorrow,
> Because He lives, my faith is strong,
> Because I know oo, He holds my future,
> And my life will go, on and on
> Because He lives.

In spite of singing the song repeatedly and thought its wording had the required effect, it did not dispel the poignant ominous foreshadowing that was gnawing my heart. I was late in thinking about marriage. Yes. No man had greeted me with ulterior motives for the three years I had been in Yaounde. Yes. No boy had made a move toward me while I was at Lourdes. Yes. I had never indulged myself in makeup in order to attract men to me. Yes. At a wedding a man danced with me and fondled me and I abandoned him. Yes. To where will all that lead? Surely, to rejection. I took two tablets of codeine to smooth my stretched nerves. The miracle came sooner than expected and I slept.

Chapter Seven

The next morning Saturday, I decided to meditate rather than work. So, I declared a unilateral holiday for the Bakery workers. I told the manageress to give the children the leftovers of whatever was in the store. She said there was too much of everything. She instead gave the children the things to go and hawk on shared dividend. They were very happy and in the evening she handed me 103,000 Frs. after giving the children their share. I gave her 30,000 Frs. from it and she went. Left alone, I started x-raying every inch of my life. I could not see any reason why I should blame myself for the calamity that loomed large in my eyes. I could not blame my parents either. If they inhabited difficult terrain, it was because that was the best they could get. So, I found myself lingering on the brow of the dreadful word **predestination**. Church teachings frown at predestination because it renders the concept of God and prayers useless. Caught in that quagmire, I took a nine day novena retreat with the last three days dry fast. The fast would end seven days to Imelda's elder sister's wedding. That would give me time to recuperate from the fast and get ready to bake the cake.

On Wednesday, third day into the novena prayers, our results were published. Imelda came to break the news. "Lady Bright, you have done wonders. You have led the class," she said and clapped her hands – sign of surprise. "What has happened?" I asked having forgotten about the expected results. "Results are out and you are first," she announced with a whim of grudge. I broke into a run to go and see. And as sure as day break, I led the class. As I ran back to meet her, I sang: Serving the living God

> I am serving the living God, amen.
>
> Serving the living God
>
> I am serving the living God, amen.

When I got to the house and continued singing and dancing, Imelda remarked, "Surely that your God has worked wonders, but stop now, I want us to discuss the wedding."

"Sister, let me dance and give thanks to my Lord, to my living God, to the almighty, to the maker of heaven and earth, to the Father, Son and Holy Spirit, to the Alpha and the Omega, to He that did great things to Sarah, to He that anointed Mary. Let me glorify Him for destroying the walls of Jericho. Let me acknowledge Him who has done and will do great wonders to me, that His name may be glorified forever, that his name may reign for ever and ever. Amen," I exulted breathlessly.

"Yes, you have every reason to thank God. Congratulations," Imelda said and embraced me. I sat down exhausted. "Yes Miss Bri, I hope you have not forgotten about my elder sister's wedding cake. The wedding is two weeks away. I have come that we do the costing and see what you need to prepare for it.

"What hue and silhouetting taste would you like – lemon, orange, lime, guava, coco nut or passion fruit?"

"Miss Bright, I beg, I don't think I have reached that level of sophistication. You merit your first. Please simplify yourself."

"I mean, what colours and what taste should linger at the background of the cake."   "I think you should choose what will sell you best. However my sister is mad with pink, blue and yellow. With taste, well, lemon."

"Ask the couple about the colours. Let us be sure. As for the cost, I think you better leave that with me."

"Lady Bright, wedding cakes cost much – as much as from 70,000 Frs. to 150,000 Frs."

"Suppose I say I have put aside 200,000 Frs. for it? What else can I do to appreciate what you mean to me?"

"Thank you very much. Now, what about *ashwabi,* the wedding uniform*?"*

"I don't think I am bound to wear the *ashwabi.* The other woman did not wear *ashwabi.* I shall wear something presentable as she did."

"OK. Please, celebrate your success peacefully. Let me leave you," Imelda advised and left. Immediately she left, I started singing 'I am serving the living God' again. I sang it, I cooed it, I hummed it and danced, and danced. I had expected a pass, not a tale-telling one. But there I was, I was only three days into my novena prayers, and the glory of God was manifesting itself. What more, when the novena would be followed up with a three day dry fast? *She who believes in our lord Jesus Christ will never die, will never remain single, will never have cause to fear, for the Lord is with her and only with her, she will never die. Come Holy Ghost, Creator come, from Thy bright heavenly throne, come take possession, of our souls and make them all Thy own. Those who believe in God, have nothing but peace, they never pine away, even in the heart of darkness.*

After reciting these hymns, I felt a new awakening, a new confidence in my Lord. Yes – a new hope. And with that, I decided to face tomorrow. To face the next day because my Lord is living. To discard makeup, because my lord is living. To stop worrying about having never been greeted by a man with ulterior motives, because my Lord is living. And in the next several days I did my novena and fasted as planned.

Most students had already left for the three months holiday. Only those who were waiting for the wedding were around. One evening, I heard one of our lecturers quarreling with three of such students because according to him, they were over staying their rents. He had evicted them but they were still stubbornly holding on. I moved to him and begged him to give the students a few days. I said once they left after the wedding, he should buy new locks and lock them out. Furthermore, I told him most landlords in Bonamoussadi especially lecturers, avoid such showdowns with tenants by handing the administration of their buildings to students. The students collect the rents and the landlord simply comes for the money at the end of the month. I said students understand themselves better. They like ridiculing and worrying landlords especially those they accuse of exploiting them. The lecturer thanked me and said when we resume I shall take over the administration of his buildings. That clicked open another business front in my mind.

Two days before the wedding, Imelda came and asked whether she should include my name in the list for makeup at her expense. I said I would do my makeup with Christ. She looked disappointed but helpless. She sighed and said she wanted me to appear cute because I was at the centre of the occasion. I promised I would be dazzling in Christ's name. She frowned and left grumbling. A day before the wedding I went to the hairdresser and asked her to choose the hairstyle that would suit my low hair. She chose pigtails. She shampooed my hair and exquisitely did the pigtails. I paid her 2,500 Frs. for it. On the wedding day, I appeared in a pleated skirt that reached well below my knees, and a loose blouse laced with sparkling beads – a sort of variegated constellation of specks. My shoes were equally simple but presentable and comfortable.

The wedding was a great success in organization and punctuality. The bride and groom trains virtually arrived the church grounds at the same time. Mass started on time. Reception was immediately after mass and the cutting of the cake which was my main concern happened when everybody was alert. When Imelda introduced me as Miss Bright the baker of the cake and lady who had assisted in setting up the cake of an earlier wedding, there was a standing ovation. I stood up bowed at the couple, the chairperson and the entire hall. Then I invited the couple to the cake stand. I arranged their standing positions then stepped aside a metre from the bride and started.

"Well, Edward and Debora, I was greatly humbled when sister Imelda told me you had chosen me, to do your wedding cake. You left renowned bakers and chose a novice. The significance of that lies in the way you chose yourselves for husband and wife. You did not go for the experienced. You went in for the inexperienced in each other. Debora's beauty is a pass-partout and she would have chosen a financial tycoon instead of a handsome young man with whom she has to start life from the scratch. Edward's handsomeness is tale-telling, yet he like his wife chose to be humble. I would have liked to present this cake in terms of its grotesque shape but I have been advised to stick to its colours. I have chosen three humble colours for you – blue, pink and yellow. Blue signifies the sky and the sea. The sky and the sea signify self-containment. Pink is a sacred colour. It signifies piety. And yellow is the colour of the Vatican - rock. You both know what being Vatican means. You are the rock on which all weddings are built. Take this knife therefore, and sanctify your union by cutting the cake made by my humble hands. Debora take hold of the knife first and Edward grip your D's hand and at the count of three – descending order, you cut. Ready, threee, twooo, oneee – cut. (Applause) Now, Lady D, show the world how you as wife and potential mother would feed your family by feeding your E. (Debora got a slice of cake and fed Edward. Then I asked Edward to reciprocate) (Standing ovation)

Imelda rushed to me and whispered, "You merit your first. Fantastic! Where did you get that wisdom?" I sulked at what I thought was a mockery of my brilliance at our exams. However, that was not the best place for quarrels. So, I put up the public face and very soon, after all other formalities, the couple were asked to open the floor. It was an emotional opening of the floor. Edward moved to the centre of the hall and raised his hands expecting his darling to just dock in.

Debora took her time in getting up from her seat. Her getting up was not just an ordinary life motion. It was a display of the art of getting up to streamline the excellence of beauty. And when she moved onto him and fitted herself into the raised hands, (like a solved jigsaw puzzle) my hitherto frozen instincts thawed and tears of pent up emotions rolled down my chicks. The MC allowed them to have the feel of each other and after a while, the music like any other thing on earth, ended and the floor was opened to the invitees.

A forest of hands came to ask me to dance with them. Nine gentlemen took turns to dance with me. Three fondled me but I did not react violently. I simply applied the lesson Imelda had implanted in me and discovered that unfaithful married men told horrible lies.

Two days after the wedding, that is, on Monday, a gentleman caught up with me on my way to the market. He stopped me and after greeting me asked whether I knew him. I said I knew him and called his name.

"You are brother Pius Ntchotu. You sing base in our church choir. I know you. I even know your compound in Bamenda."

"I am sorry sister; I didn't know you knew me so well. I just wanted to congratulate you for the marvelous presentation of your cake last Saturday at the wedding. It was fantastic. Very few women are that bold and knowledgeable. The cake itself was a tale-teller. Your dress was marveling, in fact, I lack words to describe how I felt. I am sorry. I am saying this because, you see, I see two Emerencias in one – the innocent reticent and abstemious church Emerencia and the sophisticated oratory and unrestrained occasions Emerencia. I have observed you at two weddings and to be candid, I can't reconcile. Congratulations. I am hurrying for an appointment at the Ministry of Finance. Please see you in church on Sunday," he said and hurried away. To say one has developed chickens in their heart is to say one has developed desires or worries that chirp in their heart – keeping one ill at ease. Brother Pius' encounter with me made me develop chickens in my heart. To make the choir work, we addressed each other as brother or sister – brother and sister in Christ. But out of the choir, our relationships were distant and loose. Was brother Pius' encounter to show appreciation for my brilliance a sign of wanting closer relations? If so, wasn't it to be taken as a consequence of the novena – the working of the spirit of God? Agreed, his appreciation was based on events at party halls. But he was a church person. He sang the praises of our Lord and Savior in church. "OK, I shall see him on Sunday as he had promised," I said to myself as I tried to tame my erupting nerves.

Chapter Eight

On Thursday, Imelda came to tell me that having helped her sister to settle for a week, she would be going on holiday on Saturday. I lost balance. Saturday was not good for me. Brother Pius had promised he would see me on Sunday.

"Sister Imelda," I addressed her. "Saturday is not good enough for me. Only Monday can be OK.

You see, I have to tell the congregation that I won't be around."

"OK, then we leave on Monday," she said and added, "we have already wasted two weeks here."

"We have not wasted two weeks. We have dutifully spent two weeks," I responded.

"Emerencia, I am sorry. What's the difference?" she asked.

"Waste is negative. Spend is positive," I answered. She clucked and left – leaving me to brood over undefined thoughts about seeing Pius on Sunday. On Sunday he came to church ostentatiously dressed. In singing, he was rather too loud. He seemed to be seeking prominence. After mass, I convened a short meeting in which I told the choir that I would be away on holiday as from Monday. Then I reminded those who had not completed their contributions toward a new uniform to do so before I returned. Pius paid all on the spot to the embarrassment of people who said he had denounced the idea of new uniform. When the meeting closed, somebody put up his hand and asked, "Sister Emeren, no cake?"

"If you want cake, come to my house," I responded. The whole choir followed me to my house. Since I hadn't enough space in the bakery, I distributed the cake outside. Those who got their share left immediately. Pius had however entered the house in the pretext of helping slice more cake. When the sharing was over, he stayed behind to wish me safe journey to Bamenda and to ask that I bring him something – something good. Without thought, I said he should also keep me something good. We were now left alone. With that, he moved onto me and stretched his chicks for a kiss. "What are you up to?" I asked perhaps in the crudest manner – I believe Imelda would have had a better approach. He breathed heavily perhaps from disappointment. "I shall see you when you return. How long will you be there?" he asked.

"I believe a week or two would do," I responded and he left.

On Monday we set off for Bamenda. We missed the first vehicle and so had to wait for long for another vehicle to load. To fight boredom and the uncouthness of park-boys who in hustling heavy loads to the vehicle pushed and insulted passengers, we moved away from the park and sat under a tree a good distance away. Imelda started the conversation.

"Sister Bright," she addressed me.

"Sister Emerencia," I corrected.

"OK, Sister Emerencia, my elder sister and her husband have asked me to thank you most heartily for the wonderful sacrifices and insightful presentation of your cake at their wedding. They said they least expected it and thought they would acknowledge it more formally in the nearest future," she said.

"I believe I owe them more than they owe me; unless you did not tell them how close we were. My life rotates around you. And you and your sister are not two different persons to me. May the Lord bless them," I prayed.

"Sister Emerencia, your makeup that day was not sophisticated yet it caught the eye of many a man. People are still discussing it. My sister in particular was flabbergasted by it and described it as delicate artistry. Who was your designer?" she asked.

"He who does great things to the humble," I responded.

"How much did it cost?" she asked.

"Blouse and skirt, 35,000 Frs. hairdo 2,500 Frs. and Vaseline and perfume 6,000 Frs." I responded.

"That is the cost of my inner wears. So cheap, yet so charming! Wonderful!" she exclaimed and clapped her hands.

"Sister Imelda, please before we get to the vehicle let me confide something in you. I don't like conversing in the bus especially about things that are personal and private. Some students make it the habit of vomiting their shit in vehicles to show off that they are university students – the untouchable skyscrapers. I don't like that. I would have preferred to tell you this in Bamenda but since we can't predict what lies ahead of us, I better tell you now. A gentleman met me the other day and said that he heard I was going to Bamenda. He said I should bring him something good. I responded that he should also keep something good for me."

"Where did he say he had met you before that day?"

"In church and at the two weddings."

"Did he dance with you?"

"I can't remember. But I think, no."

"Do you know him?"

"Yes. He is a member of our church choir."

"What will be your reaction if he came now and said he wanted to marry you?"

"I would ask for a six months observation period."

"Did you look at his fingers? What types of rings did he wear and on which fingers?

"He wore a ring engraved with cowboy emblems on the sensitive finger."

"Good. What do you think is your age

difference?"

"He is prettily my elder."

"Did you ask him whether he had children?"

"No. I couldn't because he did not make a concrete proposal. I am hinting you now so as to prepare your reaction once he makes a proposal. I may not see you in Bamenda. I want to spend only a few days with my parents and return to Yaounde. There are lots of commands for biscuits and cakes and other pastries."

"Yes, inasmuch as I enjoy your cakes, I shall like you to prepare to get into Ecole Normale Superieur. Cake-making brings in money but it lacks the finesse for which you have been breaking your head reading day and night. A baker's cakes can be made for the high tables but the baker himself must remain in the bakery. With your brilliance at the last exam, the summit of our being here in Yaounde, you are a sure candidate for Ecole Normale. To return to your topic, if that fellow asks your hand in marriage, don't rush to him. Avoid direct contact with him. Tell him you would be more comfortable if you communicated through a middleperson. A middleperson would unknowingly leak bits of information about him that he himself would invidiously conceal. If he is prettily your elder, he may be one of those cheats that had been impregnating girls and abandoning them, and getting to a glitch now, wants to settle with a shame-proof face at the expense of an innocent ignorant victim. Since he has not made a formal proposal, we need not exhaust our spittle on the matter," she concluded and told me it was time to move back to the park.

I plodded behind her to the vehicle completely distraught. Her questioning and concluding remarks sent me into a sort of stupor immediately I entered the vehicle. I coiled myself up into my seat and closed my eyes. Perhaps because I had told her that I disliked conversing in vehicles, she avoided waking me up. Corpses don't feel the bangs and rocking of vehicles. I was a living corpse. When we arrived Bamenda and she shook me and asked me to move out of the vehicle, I was surprised that the journey was that short. I got up, stretched myself and after thanking her and praising God for the safe journey, we parted. The effect of bemoaning her panoramic review of my encounter with Pius throughout the journey was visible in my looks. I looked crestfallen like a poorly constructed scarecrow as I climbed our precipice. What would have been a triumphant reunion with my family, especially as it was crowned with my brilliance at the exams, was reduced to forged groans of fatigue. My parents took the groans for the real thing and sympathized with me. And in that anticlimactic reunion, I went to bed earlier than expected.

I slept well the whole night but was devastated when in the morning, my two step mothers came to wake me up to inquire how I slept. I had brought them lots of gifts and customarily, they would have ululated and hugged me and danced in appreciation. But my forged groans had deprived them of that fanfare and now they were expressing their concerns. I reproached myself for allowing Imelda's cross examination of my encounter with Pius derail the fanfare of my homecoming. I picked up courage, got up and assured them that I was OK.

My father came later to inquire about my health. I told him I was fine and asked him whether he knew a person at Abakwa who sold land. I said a friend's father from Wum who wanted to buy land asked me to help look for some. My father said he himself had a plot at Abakwa near Cowfence and wanted to sell it in a bid to start a small business.

"OK, if you have land, for how much would you sell it?" I asked.

"I bought it for 100,000 Frs. about five years ago. If somebody gave me 500,000 Frs. I would take," he responded.

"OK, I will tell the man you want 600,000 Frs." I concluded.

In the afternoon, we went downtown and he showed me the place. As he returned to our compound, I went to greet the Rev. Sisters and tell them about my results. After seeing them, I went to see the manager of the bakery. I told him what I wanted to do for my parents and pleaded with him to help me disguise the buying of my father's land by posing as the buyer. He accepted and we went and paid for the land. I gave him 20,000 Frs. for that and told him he would help supervise the making of mud bricks for the building. He accepted.

Chapter Nine

My holiday with my parents was wonderful but I had to cut it short because of big business that loomed in the horizon. After three weeks only, I went and saw Imelda and told her I would be returning to Yaounde in two days.

"To your sweetie Pius!" she jeered.

"Who is Pius?" I asked, pretending to have brushed aside the Pius syndrome.

"What good thing will you take to him?" she asked, sidestepping the answer to my question.

"Ah! Pius! Whatever I can lay my hands on," I responded.

"So you actually nurse the hope of buying a gift for him? That would be a great blunder. If you buy anything for him, you will be putting everything in jeopardy. Since when did women start spearheading courtship? When you return and he asks you, tell him you don't know him, say he should introduce himself to you. Don't show you have ever seen him. Pius, Pius, where does he say he knew you? When he comes to your house, tell him people don't visit you without clearance," she said emphatically.

"Imelda, you sound bitter. I can't understand you. You are affianced. You don't want me to be affianced? You tend to jeer at me. What do you mean?" I asked.

"I am not jeering at you. I want you to be properly affianced. That is why I want you to try your luck at Ecole Normale. I don't want you to fall into a snare. But if God designated him for you there is nothing one can do to change it. You should however not start giving him gifts as if you were desperate. He should have no reason to take advantage of you. Gift-giving should start with him and not with you," she advised.

Her advice, or should I call it rebuff; plunged me into brainstorming. First, I tried to reconcile her reactions in the two situations. When I abandoned a fondler of women on the dance floor, she blamed me for being erratic and preferring what she called impotent and inconsequential candidates to the consequential one. Now that I am speculating on a consequential candidate she is preaching caution. Pius had not made a concrete proposal yet. But his inroads had the flickering of mystical blessings – he came up just after the completion of my novena prayers. From every indication Imelda was candid and blunt, but then, she was mere flesh and as such, short of the knowledge of the workings of God. My encounter with Pius had the markers of the overwhelming presence of my Lord and Savior – markers that could not be compromised. "So, I would buy a befitting present for Pius," I said in my heart and after some time, I raised my hand for a farewell handshake.

"Yes before we separate, let me remind you that I am in no way a huddle to your desires. I see you downcast, if not upset. You should not be. Step into the world of affiancing with self composure so as to ensure safety. I love you very much. You are such a beautiful girl, such an admirable girl – a girl whose self-discovery has just begun, and so a girl who has to be guided through the slippery and precarious wilderness of a wicked world. May you take my blessings with you as you return. Make sure you register for the Ecole Normale examination. God bless you sister."

Imelda's farewell almost sent me to tears. It was frank and very insightful. I left in confusion but very confident that God had my future in His hands. I had brought one million francs to Bamenda for the purchase of land. I had bought land for only six hundred thousand francs. We were in the heart of the raining season and so the moulding of mud blocks could not be started. So I opened a bank account in Cameroon Bank with the leftover money for the building project. Two days later I left for Yaounde.

The manageress of my bakery welcomed me heartily and without allowing me settle down made a report of the business.

"Auntie," she addressed me, "thank God you have returned. Commands for wedding cakes have more than quadrupled. Doughnuts and biscuits are in high demand. Even fried groundnuts that we were about to discard is big business now. In fact, I am overwhelmed. I think we have to buy new and modern equipment to cope and employ more mature hands than members of the CYM."

"That's good," I responded. "Is that all? "

"A certain uncle, I have forgotten his name, has come here thrice asking when you would return."

"What did he say he wanted me for?" I asked.

"I did not ask him. Once I said you had not returned he dashed off."

"That's OK. Let me rest. If anybody comes to ask for me tell them I am not in. OK?"

"Yes auntie," she answered.

I entered my room and lay down. Before I closed my eyes for a nap, I heard a voice – Pius' voice at the bakery. To stop the manageress from telling him that I had not returned, I called and told her, probably without thought, to tell him that I was coming. I dashed out to meet him and before I knew what I was doing, I was in his embrace.

"Welcome darling," he greeted. How was your holiday? I thought …"

"You thought what? Please leave me. Who are you? Where did you know me? People don't visit me without clearance. Please go out of my house. Next time I shall call the police…"

That sudden and perhaps insane outburst

worked on the manageress and Pius alike. She gasped and covered her mouth with both hands, and he skipped out of the house and disappeared. In fact the manageress had every reason to be stunned. She had never seen a man come so close to me and perhaps to her delight that day she saw the miracle, then she saw everything bashed and broken. I reentered my room exhausted as if I had done battle with a great demon. I slumped into my bed to think things over. I saw my blunder. It is useless crying over spilt milk. I have lost Pius – the consequence of double nature. I shall settle for what forced me to return to Yaounde.

In the morning I went and saw the lecturer who had promised to handover the management of his mini-cite to me. He had thirty rooms at 10,000 Frs. a room every month. We agreed on the terms of handing over and control, and the necessity to renovate the buildings. He gave me the leeway. I renovated the toilets, resurfaced the floors and painted the buildings in and out. Although he complained of excessive expenditure, I told him he would make more than twice what he was losing in repairs. After him, I saw another lecturer with a mini-cite of 20 rooms at the same price. I took over his too on the same conditions. I now had 50 rooms renovated waiting to be rented out at the start of the school year. Because the buildings were by the tarred roadside, I knew they would be in high demand especially by rich girls who dreaded mud in the *quartier*. With 50 rooms to manage, I rented a room adjacent to my bakery and converted it into an office and asked the manageress of the bakery to move into it to manage the bakery and the collection of rents. I then designed contract forms to be filled by potential tenants. I then advertised the rooms. By mid-holiday, all the rooms were taken at 15,000 FRS paid upfront for ten months, with a caution of 30, 000 Frs. refundable if no damage was done to the property. I gave the lecturers 5,000,000 Frs. and bagged 2,500,000 Frs. hard cash. The lecturers were extremely grateful to receive at once 3,000,000 Frs. and 2,000,000 Frs. respectively with no strain. I took my 2,500,000 Frs. and went and opened an account with Standard Chartered Bank specifically for the Real Estate Business I was now engaged in.   I now had three accounts – the bakery account, the building account and the Real Estate account.

By Imelda's decree I registered for Ecole Normale examination, sat it and passed. She too passed. A few days before the start of the school year, she returned and complained that her brother's place was too far for her to study from there. Ecole Normale entailed more work and classes ended late. She thus asked me to look for accommodation for her at Bonamoussadi. I got her a room not far from my bakery. That was the beginning of my hell.

"Sister Emerencia," she addressed me two days after she had settled in her room. "Isn't it great that we are now neighbours? I had wanted this opportunity for your own sake. And here it is at last. We are now playing our last card. I shall not say I am intruding into your affairs. Your affairs are my affairs and vice versa. God who is all powerful worked for six days and got so tired on the seventh day that, he decided not only to rest but never to work again. By deciding not to work again He commissioned what was left undone or imperfectly done to be complemented by man. Do you understand what I mean?"

"It is blasphemous," I responded.

"How can the truth be blasphemous? What I mean is that we, the girls, must complement the imperfections of our natures with makeup. As simple as that. Makeup is not only hairdo and what have you? It is the totality of female presentation of herself in public, no matter where. A well dressed woman who puts school books in a carrier bag, what is called Sacks and Motors, and goes to school as you do is not worth playing the last card. Carrier bags are meant for provision marketing. See, all girls buy schoolbags from Printania. They stylishly hang the bags on one shoulder not across their necks as you did with your self-made straw schoolbag when we were at the university. We are now in a professional school – category A2 of the Cameroon Civil Service. You should be ready to wear high heel shoes, wear long hair, change dresses thrice a day, use expensive perfumes, so as to impose your presence on people by your looks and fragrance. This is what we do, we carry along two pairs of shoes – see, these low and flexible ones I am wearing now are meant for trekking. These high heel ones in my schoolbag, see them, are meant for e e e, when I get to a formal place of contact, I change the shoes. I tie these flexible ones in a plastic bag and shove them into the schoolbag and wear something prestigious. That is what all pacesetting girls do. It is not only books that are in the schoolbag. The soul of being a girl is ever present in the bag. When you get to a place people must jingle and make other noises to acknowledge your presence. Yes. The next thing I want to ask you is how far you have gone with Pius."

"You chased him away," I snapped.

"How did I do that? I was in Bamenda."

"When I returned, he came to greet me. He embraced me. Then I remembered that you said if he made any such moves, I should ask him where he knew me, that he should introduce himself, that people don't visit me without clearance and that he should go away. And once I said that he vanished. I don't even see him in church again."

"So you did not exchange gifts?"

"No."

"What happened with the gift you bought for him?"

"I ate it myself since it was perishable."

"So, you actually bought him a gift? Horrible! Sister, you are horrible. I believe I am wasting my time with you. Don't become the stupid fly that follows a corpse to the grave," she said and sighed contemptuously and left without bidding me goodbye.

Chapter Ten

Imelda's dislike for Pius wore a mask I could not unfold. So far, he had not made a proposal. But from every indication he showed interest in me. For the three weeks I was in Bamenda, he kept coming to find out if I had returned. Then on the day I returned, he came again. I believe if I had been gentler he would have made his intentions known or hinted. So, I took another novena session to plead with my Lord and Savior to usher him back to me according to His will. Shortly after the novena, Pius resurfaced. He met me alone in the bakery practicing Imelda's how-to-do-it-yourself retouching sophisticated makeup. He moved straight onto me and not minding that I could scream, seized me and pressed his lips onto my lips. I did not whine, I did not groan, I just saw the variegated consternation of specks, some sort of fireworks sparks blasting my vision. In fact, I felt as if I was disintegrating or, should I say, dissolving in the embrace? I can't tell whether it was a long or short minute. All I can say is that Pius' embrace was so fulfilling, so passionate and so…what have you? He was as gentle as a lamb, as smooth as a bead and as pleasing as good fortune.

"I'm sorry the lipstick! Your wife will hang you," I said as he withdrew from me and sat down panting. I eyed him sideways, got a napkin for him and asked him to wipe his mouth.

"You will hang me?" he asked, his eyes brimming with … I don't know what. Do you?

"Am I your wife?" I asked with tears filled eyes.

"You don't simply want to be. That's why you treat me worse than a dog," he retorted.

"When was that?" I asked.

"The day you returned. I came to see if you had returned, collect my gift and bid you goodbye because I was going on a long mission the next day. I don't know what happened. You got so uncouth and abusive that I dashed out of your house. I returned from mission last night after doing about four months in the bush. Although I did not know how you would react, I decided to try again. How do you feel, my darling?"

"Don't you think it is uncouth and abusive to address a woman darling when you have nothing in common with her? What makes you call me darling? Where are you sailing to? I mean, what are your intentions?"

"I love you. I want to marry you. Simple."

"Is that how you approach marriage proposals?"

"You want me to step back into the 13th Century rituals of using second parties and prolonged debates and dates? The modern approach is frank talk – straightforward talk, now."

"Now you are talking. But we have to observe each other for at least six months. Within that time, I shall tell my parents about you. And I believe you would tell yours about me. You should avoid coming here directly. I shall want us to communicate through a middleperson. That will make us create a Christian distance from each other till we consummate our promise."

"What do you mean by Christian distance – distance that disguises us as non-affianced thereby giving each of us the possibility of switching to somebody else with the least opportunity? Who will choose the middleperson? Or do we choose two?"

"Christian distance is distance that avoids what we have just done – kissing to arouse sexuality. That is sin. It is not approved by the church. In relation to choosing a middleperson, you choose. One is enough. But the person should be discrete and truthful. I don't like lousy fellows. I honour my privacy."

"I'll send somebody in the evening to give you bush meat."

"That will be kind of you. You hunt?"

"I am a prospector of gold in the Eastern Province. I am just from touring the place. There is a lot of bush meat there," he said and stood up to go. And as he went, though I did not escort him, he went with me. I could feel the pangs of separation overwhelm me. I could feel the intolerable void his departure created. Yes, if God created woman out of the rib of a man, then of course she is part and parcel of him. And in being part and parcel of him, he should be by her side. And any impediment that stood on the way of that had to be fought against with all vigour. So, I took my decision to exclude Imelda in my dealings with Pius from thence on.

In the evening he sent me a well smoked porcupine. Cooking porcupine is like roasting pork – you can't avoid the spread of the aroma. If Imelda came in, she would want to know the source of the porcupine. Since I had decided to keep her out of my dealings with Pius until everything was set for the wedding, I decided to thwart her inquisitiveness by formulating a lie that I had bought the porcupine from a hawker of bush meat. With that, I sent Pius some cake and cookies and the messenger returned. I cooked part of the porcupine and kept the rest. That day, Imelda did not come. The next day, she came. When I gave her some of the porcupine she remarked, "My nephew who carries the equipments of prospectors of gold in the Eastern Province always brings porcupine. I hear there are lots of porcupines there. I like porcupine. It tastes marvelous. Have you somebody who goes to the East?"

The comment and question gagged me. I exhaled and held my breath. Could Pius be her nephew? Of course, no. And Pius could not be a carrier of equipments. A mere coincidence then? I shivered from anxiety but kept my calm. She ate without comment again. Then she said she did not know how she would handle preparations for her wedding at Easter and the impending teaching practice from 15th of February to the 30th of April. Although I had wanted her to get married and move out of Bonamoussadi, and thus leave me alone, I advised her to tell her boyfriend to postpone the wedding because there were possibilities of our being sent to schools in the Provinces. Her boyfriend refused postponing the wedding. He instead went and saw the authorities to have the two of us do the teaching practice in town. At first I did not like the idea because I feared Imelda's overwhelming influence on me.

My fears were unfounded. Preparations for her wedding humidified our concerns for Pius. Imelda was so caught up in the two engaging activities that she forgot about him. Furthermore, he was hardly in Yaounde. The only thing I heard about him was that he had gone to the East or had sent me bush meat. With that semi-permanent absence, he could not be the object of discussion. So our period of observing each other was spinning or had spun to the end without us actually observing each other. Whatever it was, there were no negative reports. Pius sent me bush meat – a sure sign of devotion to our course. And whenever I had the opportunity, I reciprocated with what I could afford.

The manageress of the bakery was fantastic at cake design. Although we used the same ingredients, the way she designed Imelda's wedding cake gave it an aura beyond description. In appreciation, Imelda agreed with me to give her the honour to present it on the wedding day. She said her presentation would not be based on colours but on the grotesqueness of the shape of the cake. Imelda and I agreed and asked her to hint us to ascertain that it was in conformity with what we thought the invitees would like to hear. When she finished we applauded.

Imelda's family in-law arrived with her wedding gown and bride maids' dresses from London. Although I had wanted to go in for my usual simple regalia, the gown I was given conformed with my desire. It was sophisticatedly sewn yet modest – modest in the sense that it did not expose what dresses are meant to keep out of public view. On the wedding day, several people opted to dance with me. I believe I danced with fifteen people with eight asking for a date. Imelda was particularly happy that I was opening up. I danced and conversed and laughed more freely than I had done in the previous weddings. However, I gave nobody a date since I was still at the heart of observing Pius. I thought even a whimsical making of another date would be double-dealing and could jeopardize what we had been nursing for about seven months. Imelda had checked out of Bonamoussadi a week before her wedding thus giving me the leeway to relate with Pius unperturbed. But where was the Pius? He had gone gold-mining. I longed for him in vain.

Three weeks after the wedding we finished our practical teaching and started preparing for the final written exam. It took two weeks. After it, I went to Bamenda to see how far the building had gone. The walls had been raised and needed roofing before the heavy rains.

I left money for the roofing materials and returned to Yaounde. We were now waiting for the results and graduation.

One day Imelda visited me chauffeur-driven. She entered the bakery and said I should drop all I was doing and listen to her.

"Lady Bri," she addressed me. "I know you are very busy – as busy as a bee. So, you don't know what is going on. Let me tell you, our unmarried colleagues are establishing fake marriage certificates with men in town in order to be posted where their husbands are, that is, here in town. If you want to remain here, and I know you will very much want to remain since your businesses are here, you should either bribe the boys in the Ministry, or fake a marriage certificate. If you don't do either of the two, be rest assured you will be sent to a distant village college. Township is for married women. You can use Pius to fake a marriage certificate."

"Sister Imelda," I addressed her, "thank you very much for the concern. Either of the two options is condoning bribery and corruption. Both are sinful and I can never succumb to them. Why do you always think that I can't obtain anything good in this world until I sinned?"

"I have not said you can't obtain good things in this world until you sinned. First of all, what do you mean by sin? I don't think you read the Bible with any understanding. Will you keep wearing a barbed gold bangle on your wrist simply because you don't want to destroy gold? And if you break it and liberate your bruised wrist will you consider that destroying gold? Furthermore, take it this way; you have a case in court that would slam you to a five year prison term if you told the truth; but you have the option of a simple lie liberating you, what will you do – tell the truth and go to prison or tell the lie and be freed? An activity that is meant for survival cannot be termed sinful. Look for any man, a trustworthy fellow who will not bring complications thereafter and establish a fake marriage certificate with him. If not, give me 500,000 Frs. and I shall go and bribe the Minister's Private Secretary to retain you here in town. What you call sin is out of the question. "

I thought things over and over again and told Imelda to give me a day to react. She said she would give me a week and left apparently in anger. I then thought that since she thought I could strike a deal with Pius, I better look for him to establish the fake marriage certificate and after that we would later sanctify our wedding in church. I thought looking for somebody else and establishing such a sensitive document was too dangerous. The person could turn out making uncalled for claims. I then went in for a frantic search for Pius. I was told he had gone to the East. Four days later, Imelda came and asked if I were ready. I took 500,000 Frs. and gave her and she went.

Three weeks later Pius returned from the East and sent word that he wanted to see me. Although I felt bad because I had already given Imelda the money, I said he could come to my house. When he came, I was shocked that he did not rush to kiss me. My pent up desires froze. He looked downcast. Something poignant, a mysterious anguish tended to gnaw at his heart. I cast a blank stare at him and with a voice vibrating with deep concern asked, "What is wrong with you? You look sick!"

"Darling, this is the seventh if not eighth month of our observing each other – a punishing seven or eight months of total abstinence and intolerable anxiety. I would have come here now to tell you that we should go and see your parents. But a terrible calamity has befallen our company," he said and pulled out a newspaper with the caption, **The Director General of the Gold Mining Consortium In the East Murdered.** "Darling with this situation, I am afraid, our company may be closed down or liquidated. And if that happens, that will be the end of me. I don't know how I can ever survive a second liquidation and loss of savings amounting to hundreds of millions of francs. Before I joined the gold mining consortium, I was a civil engineer in charge of building bridges in the East. By the time economic crises set in, the government owed me 1.2 billion. I owed the banks and my workers 950, 000,000 Frs. If the government paid me today and I paid off the banks and my workers, I would be left with a net profit of 250, 000, 000 Frs. if not more; since I have paid the banks much of what I owed them. For the past several years, the Minister of Finance has told us lie after lie. You would remember that at the early stages of our encounter I told you of an appointment I had in the Ministry. It was to discuss the modalities of paying us the money. I am talking of us because I am not alone. Other engineers have the same fate. Now with the death of the Director General of the Consortium, I am finished. That is why I have come to tell you that things may not work as we had planned. I may have to withdraw my request because I cannot uphold it. I can't talk of going to see your parents let alone, talk of being able to handle a wedding. I am sorry. But that is the truth. Since love is truth, I have no choice but to tell you the truth."

"Say you have anchored somewhere else. Be more blunt. After waiting for you for this long, you now cast me into this chasm of infinite sorrow and regret. I have heard. I wish you and your new darling God's blessings," I said, entered my room, banged and locked the door and burst into tears. As I cried I thought I was floating in a dark chasm. I became instantly, deaf, dumb and blind. Whether Pius returned noisily or quietly I can't tell. After what seemed a century, I got up to shut the door of the bakery. I ventured out of the building to have a feel of nature's bounty of fresh air. I looked up at the sky. It was full of stars and black holes. Yes, if heaven is above, then hell is below. And where was I?

Chapter Eleven

I had no need to answer the question aloud or silently. With Imelda's absence, I knew I was mistress of my new self – a self that had grown complex; a self that my upbringing did not prepare me for, a self that Pius had put at the mercy of ridicule, a self I was determined to salvage from all odds. I consoled myself with the saying, 'Every disappointment is a blessing.' To make good the blessing meant intensifying all the activities I was engaged in, before I met Pius. So, I increased Real Estate venture to 100 rooms which yielded hard handsome cash once a year. This meant that its account grew big at the start of every school year. And since I did not need its money at the time, its bankbook was permanently in my box. The bakery account did everything – feeding us, furnishing the building project and running the bakery and so, its bankbook was always in the bakery ready to be used for inputs but mostly for outputs. Because of that, I could not carry out any renovating works on the bakery. The only thing I did was I employed mature hands to enhance the work. I intensified my church activities and prayed that the God I served should give me an alternative Pius.

Our final results were favourable. On the graduation day I was shocked by the number of colleagues who came in with faked husbands – all big men in town. Most were old sugar dandies who would not cause trouble. The girls had avoided young people who could stick to the terms of the certificates afterwards. Although Imelda had said there were more women looking for men to marry than the other way round, there were very few educated women and as such, the scramble for them was very high. When it came to posting, I was retained in Yaounde; a sure sign that Imelda had bribed the Private Secretary.

At the end of the long holiday, I took up duty at Lycée de Mvog Ada. My timetable was unbelievably overcrowded. I taught 7 hours a day and while I taught, older teachers conversed and joked under shade trees. By the sixth month, I was reduced to bones. Then one of my colleagues hinted me on what to do to reduce my workload. "Just tie a bundle of money and give to **pah**," (as the Principal was called). "You will see he will cut down your workload by three quarters depending on how much you give him. He has a big voracious family with keen appetite for foreign drinks. To catch up with that, he relies heavily on bribery."

I quickly assembled 200,000 Frs. put it in an envelope and gave **pah**. He took the money dutifully and although he thanked me, I believe he thought I was late in carrying out that obligation. It seems as if after opening the envelope and seeing the content, he was flabbergasted. He came to thank me again. Over the weekend he posted a new timetable giving me 4 hours only, on Monday. That was all. On the third week, I gave him a lightweight cake. He took it home and it seems his wife liked it. The next day he ordered for some. I made them and gave him. When he drew his purse to pay, I told him not to worry. He thanked me again and said his children liked my cakes very much. Men are as slippery as mudfish. To frustrate him, or better still to put him within the limits of free cakes, I went to Bamenda and bought for his wife, so to speak, a bag of Irish potatoes, a basket of carrots and a basket of tomatoes and went and gave her. She was very thankful and addressed me daughter in his presence. And that was it. He was now my dad and his wife my mom.

With that much time at my disposal, I increased my church and bakery work – not in the slug-like manner in which I had started but in a manner akin to Imelda's dictum. I dressed gorgeously, and tried to leave a mark wherever I went. The responses proved positive but for one year no alternative Pius came. I intensified my prayers. I knew it took long for good things to come by, yet after six months, only Pius himself came brimming with hope. My heart leaped up in confused joy. "What has brought him, the mystical power of my latest novena?" For sure, what else? My body shivered as I fought against betraying my weakness. I gave him an unfussy welcome. He sat down on his own and said he was sorry that he did not inform me that he was coming. Then he exhaled loudly and said, "Emerencia, when I last came here to announce the termination of our engagement, I did not care how you would be hurt. I was blunt to a fault because I had planned to commit suicide after our encounter; reasons being that I had lost my second girlfriend to somebody else in similar circumstances when due to economic crises, the government could not pay contractors. That worked adversely on those of us who were new in the field. Contractors borrow money from banks to execute contracts and immediately the government pays them, they pay their workers and the banks and what remains is theirs. Since I could not pay my banks and workers, they seized my property and my landlord in Bastos evicted me and I was forced to patch up life in the slums. That is the type of situation I thought I was heading to again when bandits murdered the GM of our consortium. With that, I thought enough was enough. But see how God works. The bandits who killed him have all been apprehended and the 3 billion they stole retrieved from them. Read this Cameroon Post." He breathed in deeply and brought out a newspaper and stretched it to me to take. I took it and read the caption, **The Assassins of the GM of Gold Prospection in the East Arrested and Remanded in Custody.** "You would remember that in my first encounter with you I left you very unceremoniously because I was hurrying to attend a meeting at the Ministry of Finance. The meeting was in fact, a discussion on the modalities of paying government creditors. At last, the deal has been struck. And here we are. The execution of the payment will soon start. Though it would start with Douala, with the contractors who dredged the Douala Seaport, it will soon reach us. The government is serious this time to pay the internal national debt." He pulled out another newspaper with the caption, **Bright Horizon for Government Creditors**. I listened to him attentively until he said, "I have come to tell you that if you have not already anchored somewhere else, I am ready to borrow 5 million Frs. to carry on our engagement. That means we shall be extra frugal with money to be able to see your parents and carry out a modest wedding. By the time the money gets finished, I might have been paid by one of the sources."

"You need not borrow money to go and see my parents. Here is 500, 000 Frs. That is more than enough to see them," I said, moved to the room and brought the money. Pius bowed several times in receiving the money and said we shall leave for Bamenda over the weekend. On the day of departure, he showed me one million francs and said it was inappropriate for me alone to shoulder the event in Bamenda. I shrugged my shoulders in appreciation.

We got to Bamenda, saw my parents, carried out what tradition demanded and returned to Yaounde to ask the Rev. Father to start reading our wedding banns in church. The church went hilarious when they heard that I was getting married. From then on, gifts poured in. Pius had talked of a restrained wedding but the zeal with which people received the news indicated that we could not avoid a tale-telling wedding. At the third and last reading, Imelda came to congratulate me. She said she had gone to Bamenda and heard the reading of the banns in church. She said if I had harkened to her advice and made a marriage certificate with Pius, we would not have lost 500,000 Frs. bribing the Private Secretary of the Minister of Education. I told her the loss of the money was paltry by comparison with her approval of the wedding. Before she left, she promised hiring the hotel of our choice for the reception and providing the wedding car. That was already a third of the envisaged expenditure. Help came from many other angles mostly from my customers and the church. The programme was simple. We had first to do the Civil Registry wedding at 8 o'clock on Saturday then move to church for the church wedding at 11 o'clock and start reception at 4 o'clock in *Hotel de Bonne chance.*

At the *Mairie* the mayor lectured us on the ethics of good marriage. After that, he asked us what property regime we wanted. Neither of us understood what that meant. Then he explained that there were two types of regimes – the joint and the individual. The joint was the regime in which property was jointly owned by the couples no matter who worked for it, while the individual was the regime in which property was owned exclusively by the partner who worked for it. Neither the man nor the woman had rights over the other's property, unless it was unequivocally so declared in a will later. He then asked which of the regimes we would prefer. Pius looked at me. I looked at him. He shrugged his shoulders and asked me to decide. I said joint. He confirmed. Then the Mayor asked what marital regime we wanted – polygamy or monogamy. Pius chose polygamy. I said that could not work because it was against the teaching of the church. He said in church, we would sign for monogamy. We debated for some time before he gave in. After signing the marriage certificates we left for the church where we were given another lecture before signing the church marriage certificates.

As we left the church, the CYM and other church groups sang and waved flyers with captions – Our Mama Bright, God bless you; Lady Bri weds P.; Our dear E weds P.; Lord, pour abundant graces on Mama E.; Good luck Emerencia; We love you Miss Bright; Lady Bright forever; Long live E&P.; Be blessed sister Bri.; Sister Emeren, God be with you. I was so overwhelmed by such outpouring of well wishes.

The reception was a success story. Imelda and some colleagues were wonderful. I lack words to express what they did. The Rev. Father remarked that he had never seen a wedding of that magnitude. Pius was struck dumb by the enormity of the wedding and the little he had contributed to it. He gasped and whispered, "All this is in your honour. You are great my darling." I smiled and responded, "As you make your bed so do you lie in it."

Chapter Twelve

Pius' two-bedrooms and a parlour house could not contain the gifts we got from well-wishers. So, I put some in the bakery and asked the manageress to move into my room at Bonamoussadi. The other gifts, I divided into two. Those I was to put into immediate use, I left them in our house and the others I distributed to relatives who had attended the wedding. The first year of our marriage was wonderful. Pius was by my side and sometimes even came to give a helping hand in the kitchen. He never entered the house without coming to kiss me. I became addicted to kissing which I had abhorred at first as unhygienic. After all, there was only one mouth in the entire world for me to kiss and that was, his'.

As the year wore on towards Christmas, I started getting worried. I had expected to be pregnant within the first few months of marriage. But nothing was happening. Imelda was expecting her third baby. She had told me that she wanted four, and after that, stop to enjoy the bounty of God's mercy. I told Pius about my worry. He said I should have faith in God. Six months into the New Year, nothing seemed to be happening. I became impatient and told Pius I had to see a gynecologist. He discouraged me and talked of a couple that stayed for four years without an issue but when they started having children, they needed the intervention of a gynecologist to help them stop. With that, I calmed down.

Before our graduation at Ecole Normale, we had processed all our documents for integration into the Civil Service. Because I was preoccupied with my bakery and Real Estate businesses and had no urgent need for money as my colleagues had, I did not follow up the documents. Thus, by the time their unpaid salaries accumulated into what we called **gros lot** and they were paid, I had not begun following my documents. Following, running or chasing documents in Cameroon means moving from office to office bribing your way through as you beg and sometimes physically fight with bribe-mongers for your documents to be processed. I had abandoned mine in the Ministry of Education. Only by the grace of God would they move to the Ministry of Finance for payment without my following up. But I was confident the Ministry would one day pay. I had indicated in my documents that my civil service financial transactions should be with my Real Estate Bank Account. This implied that my salary and subsequent *gros lot* would be paid into my account in Standard Chartered Bank.

One Sunday, Pius and I went to church and sat side by side. I had a cold, so I did not go to conduct the choir. A visiting Priest apparently influenced by couples' complaints, gave a sermon on marriage. He likened marriage to a journey on a straight road with the destination in the form of a building visible straight ahead of the traveler. But whenever the traveler moved one step forward, the destination took two steps backward, thus creating more distance. And by the time the traveler realized that the destination was unattainable, they were too old to question, and they died without knowing why they undertook the journey. "My dear Christians, your husband, your wife, is that destination. Verily, verily none of you will understand the other in your lifetime because as you move forward to get close to understand your partner, he/she moves backward creating more distance. Marriage is perseverance. The destination is straight ahead but you can't attain it. Go then in the peace of our Lord Jesus Christ and pray that he gives you the grace to persevere."

To me the sermon was sacrilegious. It neutralized everything around - the counseling of couples at both the *Mairie* and the church during the signing of marriage vows, and prayers for God's guidance and protection. "Is marriage a lifetime punishment?" I asked myself in my heart and brushed the sermon aside with the belief that if it were, it was for other couples not for Pius and me. I saw our whims and caprices more for better than for worse.

We were now entering the third year of marriage. Since I was automated by childhood upbringing, I left for work either to school or bakery and returned as routine. As long as there was money for the house-girl to buy provision, and of course there was money, I derived satisfaction in my work. The only thing that disturbed me was keeping to Imelda's standards of being cute even as a married woman. I had the money and so bought the dresses and cosmetics for makeup. I dressed gorgeously well and received her high rating. But she came time and again to instruct me on what to do, where, when and how.

"Madam Bri," she would call me and lecture, "when going to church, party or any formal place with your husband don't move abreast with him. Move a little ahead for him to admire your backside; and you have the most ideal one. Move in short quick shuffling steps, especially if you are in high heels. When he says something, pretend you did not hear, swerve backward at 30 degrees so that he catches a glimpse of only half your face, run the back of your left hand across your forehead as if trying to train your hair, or flick your head like this, as if to swing your hair to one side, then say something in very low voice. He will quicken his pace and ask, "What?" At that time your perfume now confederated with your natural fragrance, distinguishes you from all other users of the same perfume and overwhelms his sense of smell to stretch his nerves taut. He will then ask again, "What did you say?" At that time you swing your head like this, as if a fly had settled on your brow and you were frightening it away.

Murmur a few Americanisms and you will see what impact you are making on him. That is what is called, **fixing**. **Fixing** is creating and gluing an overshadowing image of you in him, an image he would unconsciously use as a gauge to evaluate any other woman in church or party. Once you succeed in gagging his senses with the image, there is no gainsaying. He becomes your puppy. I tell you, from master to puppy. But let me warn you, it should be a short distance trip. Never undertake a long journey in high heels. It will be counterproductive."

"Sister Imelda," I would address her and respond, "You are making the whole thing look like a pantomime."

"A pantomime! You are kidding. It is not a joke. What I am saying is called, **sustainable management** of marital relationships. Unfortunately the use of cars even in short distances nowadays is destroying that artistic and soothing aspect of marriage. There is nothing as ugly as a couple sitting in a car. A car makes them look straight ahead like birds in the wind. They lose the human touch and whosoever drives, pays more attention to the vehicle than to the partner. What a shame! **Sustainability** means, consciously putting in place checks and balances. It is the art of engraving what you are, in the mind of your husband. Don't kid in making sure that what belongs to you is yours. Some women believe that the fight for a husband ends at the wedding altar. And soon after they wed they abandon makeup and other acts of fixing. That's bad. The contest for a husband starts from betrothal and ends in the grave. Sustainability is not only on the side of the woman. Men also fix but their fixing is not as demanding as that of the woman. Their fixing is much more on whether they can provide for, and protect the family. Yes, that is it. You don't get married today and lose your husband to another woman the next day because you disregard fixing. You see, sister, losing a husband does not necessarily mean divorce. No. The most torturous loss of a husband is when another woman's image dispels yours from his heart and your physical presence becomes a malignant sore at which he sighs with contempt."

"Sister in all this you don't advocate bleaching. I have never seen you try to change your colour. And you have never advised me to change my colour. See, I am very black and I thought one of my problems in the early days was my colour. Why is bleaching not ideal?

"Makeup is enhancing what you are. Bleaching is destroying what you are. I enhance what I am with agreeable oils and not corrosives. Bleachers use corrosives to destroy what they are. Some go as far as swallowing dangerous steroids to become white. Bleaching is the apex of inferiority complex – a look low on black colour. Try red polish on black shoes. What do you obtain? A muddled nondescript ugliness.

Apply black polish on black shoes and you have the shine no other shoe colour can give. Fantastic."

"Sister, suppose one does all that and there is no favourale response from her husband?"

"What to you is an unfavourable response? Before you get engaged in fixing, study your husband's reaction to situations. Some husbands are slow, some are reticent, some are conservatively proud and others are simply insensitive and downright stupid. For such, don't just bother yourself. If they look right, you look left. But for those worth the salt, once you know what they are, you go on. Try several methods to panel-beat them. One would succeed."

Chapter Thirteen

Every day, Pius carried a portmanteau of files to the Ministry, so to speak, and returned either grumbling that the Minister had travelled without signing their documents for payment or that the case of the slain GM was adjourned once more. That had been going on for most of the time since our marriage. It meant nothing to me.

One day he came home brimming. "Darling, there is now light at the end of one of the tunnels. The court has decided that the workers of the consortium be paid fully with the retrieved money while the case of murder against the bandits is pursued normally. I would suggest then that we open a joint bank account since we chose the common ownership of property regime. This will make me ask the paymaster to send my money directly to the account. It is dangerous to handle huge sums of money even in church."

My Bakery Account Booklet had only 4 million Frs. in it. Since it was always around, I doubt whether Pius had not taken interest in it and known its contents. I had completely forgotten about my Real Estate Account with more than 8 million Frs. in it because I never thought of it until the school year began.

"We need not open another account," I said, handed him the Bakery Account Booklet, and suggested that we could go and update it with his name and signature.

"Darling!" he called rather exclaiming. "This is a savings account. It operates on the basis of one carrying money to the bank, placing it on the counter, counting it there with the counter attendant and he/she doing the entries manually. That is dangerous. You see, you don't know. Carrying huge sums of money anywhere is dangerous. That is why it would be prudent for us to establish an account into which my salary and yours will flow automatically at the end of the month.

"But you are not working. How will you have a salary?" I asked with a tint of anger. "I shall be reinstated. Our company will soon be reopened and we the senior staff will, if lucky, move up to fill the posts of the expatriates who stupidly left the country as a precaution," he responded

The next day, we withdrew 3 million Frs. from my bakery account and opened a current account in Meridian Bank. He asked for my matriculation number and the references of my documents in the Ministry of Education. I gave him the number and references and thus set him on the move. Every day, he went to the Ministry to follow up. At a certain point, he got to a hitch. The documents were missing. The lady who last handled them had retired and her table taken over by a man who disorganized everything. So, I was asked to make new documents to start from the scratch. That did not bother me. I made the documents at my pace though Pius wanted me to abandon every other work and hurry up with the documents. Two months later, I gave him the documents and he started following them from door to door in the Ministry. That became his preoccupation. He never went to the East anymore, never complained anymore about the President spending more time in Europe than in Cameroon and never talked anymore of the GM's murder and the court's decision to pay them fully. That never bothered me. I did not even realize that there was a serious situation in the making.

One day he told me that he was tired of following up the documents and as such, had bribed the Private Secretary of the Minister of Education to follow them up. He said he had given him 100,000 Frs. Two weeks later he said the Private Secretary told him the documents had finally been sent to the Ministry of Finance for payment. He said he got the references from him and dashed to the Ministry of Finance. To hasten up things there too, he bribed a gentleman who claimed to be the brother of the Minister. He said he gave him 100,000 Frs. and promised him 30% of the *gros lot – a gros lot* whose amount he did not know. The man promised with an oath that in less than a month the money would be out.

When Pius went to the Ministry at the end of the month, he neither saw the man nor could he trace where he had left the documents. The documents had disappeared once more. That day Pius returned with a scrofulous face and started bullying me for being negligent. He derided me saying when my friends were following up their documents I was making cakes. Now they had received their *gros lots* and bought cars and I was still making cakes that took me to nowhere. He insulted me and likened me to my father's compound – a non-productive wasteland, and stormed out of the house without eating. I felt the bite of the insult overwhelm me. Pius was married to me, not to my father. He could insult me, not my father. I counted the stars in the heavens. I x-rayed my situation with him – for nearly four years of marriage Pius had never given me one frank for food, one frank for soap, one frank for anything. (I was used to that. I never saw my father give his wives). I thus concluded that I was my father's wasteland because for nearly four years of marriage I could not conceive.

For two days Pius did not return. At first I tried to brush his disappearance aside as a non-event. But when I thought that he had told me that he once attempted to commit suicide, my hair stood on end and I started a frantic search for him. We take several things for granted until an issue crops up. For nearly four years of marriage, Pius had never shown me a man of substance as his friend. Even the fellow who had acted as our courtship middleperson was not worthy of the role. But so long as he was by my side and played the role of a manufacturer of babies that was fine with me. Now, where do I look for him? My only option was the church. I went and complained to all the groups in church.

"Ha! If it is him, he is at Mami Yo," one woman said contemptuously.

"Who is Mami Yo, madam?" I asked trying to mitigate the contempt.

"That Chicken-Parlour woman," she responded with a sinister folding of the forehead.

"Madam, can you take me there?" I asked with loving concern.

"It is not difficult to trace. I shall describe the place and you can get there without asking," she responded again with unmitigated degree of contempt."

She then described the place and I got there. I met Pius, my Pius, sprawled on a sofa with the left leg resting on the floor and the right flung over the backrest, the head resting on the hand-rest, his mouth wide open as he breathed through it with ear-splitting guttural snoring noise like the crackle of the exhaust-pipe of a diesel engine, terribly drunk. I gasped out of shame and sealed my face with both hands. I blamed myself for being the cause. But no, I wasn't the cause. If Pius had resorted to drunkenness because I did not follow up my documents, then he was wrong. They were my documents not his. They would have been processed before we got married. And although we were married on joint ownership of property regime, they were still mine until they yielded the joint property. Mami Yo was not at home. It seemed as if Pius had been a nuisance and everybody had abandoned him there. I also abandoned him there and returned to the house.

In the evening, he returned as if nothing had happened. He ate and went to bed. I never asked him anything. In the morning next day, I went to the bakery very early. The withdrawal of 3 million Frs. from its account was affecting its running and that of my household. Flour and other ingredients were in short supply and the turnover was diminishing. To salvage the business, I went to the Meridian Bank to withdraw 1.5 million. To my surprise, I met only 500,000 Frs. in the account. Pius had withdrawn 2.5 million; what for? And how and where did he spend the money? I developed instant palpitation, dashed out of the bank, got a taxi and got home. Pius was not there. I waited for him almost most of the morning but he did not return. I went to the bakery and assisted the manageress to do the little we could do for that day.

In the evening, Pius did not return. I did not bother myself going to Mami Yo. Next day, Thursday morning, I went and complained to the Rev. Father. He invited us in writing to his office on Sunday after

Mass. I went to the house and gave the invitation to the house-girl to give him if he came in my absence.

Chapter Fourteen

On Sunday after Mass, Pius and I went to see the Rev. Father. I narrated my story and said I wanted to know where he had put my money. A debate as to who owned the money ensued. We finally agreed that we both owned the money and as such, neither of us would have withdrawn such an amount without letting the other partner know. Pius brought out a receipt to show that he had lent out the money at 50% interest to a friend whose merchandise was stuck at the Douala port. In other wards he was expecting 3,750, 000 Frs. from the friend in a month – what he said my bakery and my salary could not produce in two months. The Rev. Father then counseled us to be faithful to each other and reconcile. He advised Pius against drunkenness and abandonment of the marital home and told him to apologize to me. Pius knelt down and in kissing my feet, promised he would never engage in any act that would displease me again. The Rev. Father then led us in a renewal of marriage vows prayers. After the prayers Pius held me and we returned home.

I could not refuse reconciling with my husband. I wanted a child – I was gradually slipping out of the convenient childbearing age. My colleagues were on their third or fourth child. I had not even begun and that was my greatest worry. Pius and I were in the heat of a revisiting honeymoon. We glued ourselves together in prayers and action. Our love bobbled. In the prime of it and perhaps seizing the opportunity it offered him, he called me and said, "Darling, I am sorry that something has been boggling my head for some time. I should have told you this long before now, but because I thought I had another solution to it, I thought since it did not concern you, it was needless displeasing you with what did not concern you. The truth about me is that I have two children. The first one is the son of my would-have-been first wife – the first girl I had wanted to marry. But when her parents found that she was pregnant, they told me to hold on, until she gave birth before paying the bride-price. Unfortunately for me, she passed away in childbirth leaving the child. My aunt then took custody of the child. The second case is the one I told you that when the government was unable to pay contractors, I lost my girlfriend to somebody. She had given birth to my child and we were getting ready to marry, when that calamity hit the nation. So, my aunt took charge of the second child also. I go to the village time and again to see the children but let me tell you frankly, I only escape at night to thwart their insistence that I bring them to Yaounde."

"What was that your other solution to the

problem?" I asked with a trembling voice.

"Since in both cases I did not pay bride-price on their mothers, I thought of returning the children to their maternal families. That is our tradition," he responded.

"I think that is gross irresponsibility. You abandon the care of your children to an old aunt and at a given time return the children, your blood, to their maternal families, then look for a sweet wife and enjoy life with her. Please, Pius go and take those children immediately and bring them here. We are condemned to give them a Christian education and let them have the feel of people who care," I said, wiped the sweat off my brows and left him.

Four days after Pius had brought the children, I got word that my mother was sick. Knowing she was in dire need of help, I took off for Bamenda immediately. I met her very sick and took her to hospital. She was diagnosed with typhoid. I bought the drugs and after some time, she picked up. I noticed that she eyed me strangely. When I enquired why, she said she was surprised that I was still as dry as a dry season twig. I told her I did not understand it myself. I said my husband and I have done everything we could but nothing was happening. She asked what we had done so far. I said just working for it. She asked whether we had seen a medical doctor. I said no. Then she groaned, got her walking cane and plodded out of the compound. In the evening, she came in with an elderly woman – a traditional gynecologist. The woman examined me and made a concoction of herbs and gave me.

"When you return to Yaounde, dilute this in a bit, very little lukewarm water and administer enema to yourself morning and evening for six days. Make sure that the water is very little so that you don't defecate immediately after the enema. Don't miss a day even if you heard that your mother was dead. When the treatment is done, buy biscuits and groundnuts if you don't have money, if you have money, cook and make a small feast for the children of your compound. When the children finish eating and are returning to their homes, carry the youngest ones out of your house and when you get outside, give them sweets, then return to your house and enter your room. You will see," she advised.

"*Mami*, should I abstain from e, e,e when taking the treatment?" I asked.

"No, why? You should not," she responded.

"How much should I pay you for this?" I asked.

"Nothing. The spirits forbid me from taking any money or gifts from my patients. But if things work out well they are free to give me whatever they have," she responded.

That response put me in a difficult situation. Seeing the distance she had covered in coming and would cover again in returning, seeing how devoted she was, I thought she needed a little compensation whether what she stood for was logical or not. So, I called my mother outside out of earshot of her and asked her what she thought I should do. She advised that whenever I would be returning to Yaounde I should leave whatever I have with her and she would give it to her at a convenient time well after my return. With that we returned to the house and after a brief while we suggested it was time for her to return.

She readily got up and we set off to escort her. When we got midway, she asked whether we were taking her right to her compound. She advised that we return. In bidding us goodbye she shook hands with my mother and when it came to my turn, she held my hands and said, "The gift I want from you is greater than money; if all goes well, and I believe it will, name the child after me if it is a girl or after my husband if it is a boy." In releasing my hands she said, "God bless you." Immediately she said that, what I had taken for a casual human interaction seemed to have received spiritual anointing. I experienced a sudden uplifting. My heart swelled with undefined gratitude to her. I thought I had moved a step forward toward my desire. Yes, the way she said it, her saintly whims and self-denial made me convinced she meant business. She turned and started plodding away; and as my mother and I stood watching her lumber toward a bend, we unconsciously raised our hands and voices to stop her from going, but with her mission accomplished, so to speak, she paid a deaf ear to us and we watched with shuddering helplessness as distance swallowed her up.

From then on, I was in the full grip of her aura and that made me develop thoughts of immediate return to my husband. By the time we got home I had taken my decision to return to Pius in two days. I was confident I was a new Emerencia.

I met Pius very anxious and very welcoming. Although I did not tell him about the traditional treatment, I found a new spirit in him. His children had missed me very badly. They came to embrace me calling me mama. I coddled them in return and showered them with gifts of sweets they had been deprived of in childhood. My household population now stood at five. Two extra mouths to feed. That did not matter, so long as my Pius was around me. Whenever I made a hind-view of our situation I could hardly say with certainty what actually led to Pius' despondent behaviour. So, I thought I had not taken fixing seriously and therefore another woman's image had infiltrated into him. To dispel it, and make him wholly mine, I put into practice 'Imeldaisms'.

Time and again I invited him for a stroll; walked abreast with him for awhile, then skipped ahead for him to admire my backside. And while I moved in front of him in short shuttling steps, I spoke some Americanisms, listened to hear him ask, "what?" swerved at 30 degrees for him to catch a glimpse of only half my face, tried to see whether I made any impact, but in the end, I would sulk from utter disappointment as I would neither hear him ask nor see him pay attention to me. I would instead see him gazing at something else, his thoughts a thousand kilometers from me.

Two months had passed since I returned from Bamenda and Pius had made no mention of the 3.75 million he was expecting from his friend. I feared asking him to avoid breaking the rhythm of our new found intimacy. All I wanted from him was a baby. In the third month, I started having constipation and nausea. The situation worsened by the minute. I told Pius to accompany me to hospital. When we got there the doctor diagnosed that I was two months pregnant and gave a prescription. As usual, Pius watched me buy the drugs and brace myself for motherhood.

About two months after that, the cankerworm struck again. For no apparent reason, he took interest in my documents again and went to the Ministry of Finance to trace them. From every indication, he met the person he had bribed and promised 30% of the *gros lot*. The fellow, probably aggrieved that he had lost the 30% of the *gros lot*, told him the money had been paid but did not say into which account it was paid. He instead called the police for him. Pius escaped arrest by sneaking out of the fence before the police arrived.

When he got home, he dashed straight at me and bellowed, "Emerencia, you think you are smart? You got the money and made me move up and down chasing the wind? Where have you kept it? You fool."

he insulted and gripped me by the throat. The children screamed.

"Which money are you talking about?" I managed to croak.

"The *gros lot*," he responded still gripping me by the throat virtually strangulating me.

"Yours or mine? And you brutalize me for my money? Where have you put the 250,000, 000 Frs. the government owes you? Where have you put the 3,750, 000 Frs. you expect from your friend? What about your gold prospection money? You abandon all that and chase after *gros lots*? How much can a teacher's *gros lot* amount to? If as you say the money has been paid, then I think it has not been positioned into our account. You need go to the bank again and check. I have received no money. I swear to God, I have received no money."

My vehement swearing might have worked on him. He let go my throat and sat down. The children flashed wild angry glances at him. The house-girl was so shocked that she started crying. I got up calmly and moved to the room and wept bitterly. He might have heard me hiccoughing intermittently and so could not enter the room to face the outcome of his brutality. He went out and only returned when he thought I might have slept. He knocked at the house-girl's window and she opened the door for him.

Immediately he entered our room, I was overwhelmed by the nauseating stench of stale vomit.

He locked the door and with shoes on, slumped into bed beside me. He farted once, twice and in the third, I leaped out of bed, dashed out and bolted the door to make him inhale the content of his septic tank. It was horrible. It seems as if after inhaling a good dose of it, he was suffocating and wanted to jump out. He knocked at the door violently. He punched it and perhaps used his shoes to hit more violently but I refused to open. In the morning, the house-girl opened the door for him and he attacked me on the sofa where I had passed the night. Believing that he would be restrained by the taboo against brutalizing pregnant women, I took a stool when he gave me the first slap and threw it at him. It hit him on the head and bruised it. He yelled and came in with what I would call a premeditated intension to kill. He threw a boxer's punch. It caught me straight in the face and sent me sprawling helplessly on the floor. He fell on me and dragged me in between the chairs and started kicking me on the stomach. I shouted, "Pius, Pius, your child is in that stomach. Your child is in that stomach. He kicked on remorselessly, below the belt; he kicked on and on smashing and pounding with his heels, when I realized he was surely trying to destroy with sinister intent something he did not want…"

I cannot say for how long I remained unconscious. When I regained consciousness, I found myself in hospital. The house-girl was fanning me. I asked her why I was in hospital. She said, "Because uncle beat you unconscious. When he was beating you, I ran to call neighbours. Before they came you were barely breathing. So they carried you to this hospital."

At that time, my senses were numbed. I felt no pains, even my swollen lips did not pain and so I thought I was OK. I returned to the house, picked a few things and went to pass the night at the bakery. The house-girl and the two boys waited for Pius to return to the house in the evening but he did not. Late at night they braved the distance and joined me at the bakery.

After two days at the bakery, I developed excruciating pains all over my body but most awfully in the stomach. I soon realized that I had traces of bleeding. I went to the gynecologist who had diagnosed my pregnancy and told him my story. He said I might have had a rupture. And when he x-rayed me, he confirmed. He then put me on total bed rest and prescribed very expensive drugs. I bought and took them. In spite of that, the bleeding continued unabated. On the fifth day of bleeding, I aborted twins. My tears were beyond measure as I saw my world end before my eyes. The doctor did everything to console me and save me from further complications. In his presence I promised I would forgive Pius but deep down me, I thought of revenge.

Chapter Fifteen

Immediately I was discharged from hospital, I went and saw the Rev. Father and told him my story. I told him I wanted immediate divorce.

"Emerencia," he addressed me, "the church does not grant divorce on demand as you advocate. In situations like yours, the church counsels the couples and in most cases makes them reconcile. Pius is human. He can change to become a caring and loving husband. So, please, calm down. I shall invite him and talk to him again."

"Father, for you to marry him, or for me to marry him?" I asked, almost scolding the Father.

"For you to reconcile with him. Remember the marriage vow – you vowed you would live by and for each other for better or for worse, till death did you part."

"Father I have not come here for moralization lessons. I have come here for you to declare divorced Pius and Emerencia now, whether he is present or not. And if you continue with your moralization lessons, I shall pronounce the divorce and walk out. The Bible does not say a woman shall live by and with a murderer for better or for worse."

"Emerencia, what you are saying may be logical but falls short of the teaching of the church. Take heart. Whenever I lay hands on Pius, I shall talk to him and you will see a changed and loving husband."

"Father, there is no lesson I can learn from you. You have never been married. You have never been barren. You have never been cured of barrenness. You have never suffered from brutal beating. You have never aborted twins and so, you can say nothing tangible when it concerns experiences you have never gone through. **In the name of our Lord Jesus Christ, I pronounce divorced Pius Ntchotu and Emerencia Chungong**." I pulled off the wedding ring from my finger and placed it on the Father's table. "Here is his wedding ring. Return it to him as the celebrant of our wedding and if you like, tell him to return mine or throw it in a pit latrine." I then walked out. He called me back several times but I moved away. The next day I went to court to seek court divorce too. I got a lawyer, told him my story, gave him the medical certificates and pictures of my battered face, and money for court charges. He did not only file for divorce he filed for damages too. The court then issued a search warrant for Pius who had not been seen since he nearly killed me. Three weeks after the search warrant, we published the pending hearing in the National Gazette and two other daily newspapers. Three months elapsed; Pius did not appear in court.

The divorce was upheld as requested by the aggrieved party in the absence of the accused. Emerencia Chungong and Pius Ntchotu were declared divorced by the court.

At that time, the economic crisis was biting hard. One of the lecturers whose *mini cite* I was administering advertised it for sale because he wanted to migrate to the United States of America. I loved it but thought I hadn't enough money. He wanted 25, 000,000 Frs. for it. I at once thought of my Real Estate account. I knew I had a little above 8,000,000 Frs. in it. I thought if I sold the bakery, I could raise as much as 15,000,000 Frs. but would the seller accept part payment? I rushed to the bank, and lo and behold! My seven years arrears had been paid into the account and I had 27, 000,000 Frs. in the account. I beat down the price of the *mini cite* to 20, 000,000 Frs. and paid the lecturer cash. It was a 20 rooms building. I renovated four for my personal abode and gave out sixteen to students. While Pius was still in hiding, I transferred all my belongings to the last pin from his house to my new abode. I tried to make his children and the house-girl remain behind but they all followed me.

Pius finally resurfaced when he thought time had healed the wounds. He got to his house and met it as empty as it was before we got married. We had replaced his old furniture with my new furniture when we got married and packed his old woodwork at the veranda. We put back his old stuff and carried away my furniture including the bed. He might have been shocked to the bone when he returned and saw what had happened. He asked of our whereabouts, he was told and he followed, believing with the wrong face of logic that he was still my husband. He entered the house, saw its standard and asked where the master of the house was. I told him I was the mistress of the house and ordered him out. When he resisted, I called the police. They arrested him for breach of the peace and took him to the police station. There, he told the police that I was his legally married wife and showed them both our church and Civil Registry wedding certificates. I countered that with the court judgment approving divorce as requested by the aggrieved party in the absence of the accused, who was fully informed of the pending judgment by gazette and newspapers, but who failed to show up at the hearing thereby being guilty of contempt of court.

The ASP was confused. "Madam, this is a family case. The two of you should go back home and reconcile your differences. Mister, I see here that you beat your wife causing her injuries. Look at the medical certificate. Whoever told you that men beat their wives these days? If we had caught you, you would have been locked up in cell one for one week to teach you a lesson. Go and apologize to your wife. I see; she is very angry. Please use intermediaries to appease her. Madam, two wrongs don't make a right.

If he apologizes, please, forgive him. The two of you should go."

"Mr. ASP, I am returning to my house. I say my house. He should return to his. I don't want any reconciliation," I said and dashed out of the police station. I stopped briefly to talk to a friend. It may be Pius overtook me then. By the time I entered my house, he was there. I ordered him out and told him he was inviting the wrath of vengeance upon himself. He walked out but returned the next morning to accuse me of stealing some of his property. He skipped our Bonamoussadi police station and went to the Central Police Station and laid the complaint of abandonment of the conjugal home, and embezzlement of conjugal property in the process. He might have bribed the police because when they came, they menacingly bundled me into their van without telling me what crime I had committed, whizzed me off to their station and locked me up in the filthy cell one – the cell of hardened criminals. It may be the ASP in charge of the cells was not on duty for two days. On the third day, in the morning the ASP *Centrale* opened the cell, and there before him, I emerged emaciated. He peeped at me and shrugged his shoulders trying to recollect where he might have seen me before. He sort of recollected fast and asked, "Madam, where did I once see you? What's your name?"

"We met at Imelda's wedding. I am Lady Bright, the lady who makes wedding cakes."

"And what brings you here?" the ASP asked.

"I don't know," I responded.

"*Element*," he addressed one of the policemen standing by, "this lady says she does not know why she was brought here. What have you to say?" the ASP asked.

"Her husband accuses her of abandoning her conjugal home and stealing property in the process," the constable responded lightheartedly.

"Madam, who is your husband?" the ASP asked.

"My former husband," I corrected.

"You are divorced then?"

"Yes."

"Can you bring the divorce documents?"

"Yes. I can dash to the house and bring them," I responded.

"Jean-Paul," he called a boy from his office and asked him to take a nearby vehicle and drive me to my house and back. I entered the vehicle and within a short time we returned. When he saw the documents he clucked, shook his head, pouted and lashed out contemptuously, "Madam, what is wrong with you women? How comes that you .chose to marry a fey man – a fellow who carries the equipments of gold prospectors from camp to camp in the East? That fellow is a wanted criminal."

I shuddered with embarrassment at what the ASP had said. His remarks clicked-opened my mind. I saw in the blur of time, why Pius, always ostentatiously dressed and tall-talking, chose to live in a virtually rent-free house in a ghetto. He had no need for a decent habitat. No doubt, he was always on the move. His house was a den where he rested to plan his prowling. If it were what it looked like during our wedding, then for sure, it was worse before the wedding. He might have just given it a facelift for the occasion. No doubt his furniture; what an antithesis!

"But Mr. ASP," I interjected with a quivering voice, "he said he was an engineer turned geologist prospector of gold in the East,"

"Those are lies they tell you women and you fall headlong for them. Where did he say he studied – in Britain, America or Russia? Let him go and sleep. He is a wanted man. He was once a money swindler. To escape arrest, he moved to the East where he became a labourer with Nanga Company in bridge construction. Even there, he swindled and was thrown out. Then he became a carrier of the equipment of gold prospectors. If my junior staff had known that, he would have been arrested immediately he came here. I am sorry for the inconveniences we have caused you. Please return to your house. He will not dare come here again if he hears that I am in charge here. If he does, he will be detained."

I got home soaked with sweat boiling hot, bubbling with rage. The only befitting option I had for Pius was to fight back. He had murdered my twins so he deserved death in return. He had to be eliminated for several offences – the misuse of my money, attempt to murder me, the brutal murder of my twins thereby depriving me the honour of fulfilling the pledge to name my children after the native gynecologist and her husband, and the torture I underwent at the police station.   Worse still, he brought to zero the jump-start I would have made in childbearing. Can you imagine that! Bullshit, he must pay with his life.

I nosed around and got two thugs and told them I wanted them to help me eliminate him. They stretched out their hands and asked for 1.5 million. I beat it down to 0.5 million and stood my ground. We argued and finally agreed on, upfront payment of 0.5 million. I suggested we sign a document as guarantee. The elderly of them insisted on a verbal deal and assured me of their professionalism. Just when I capitulated and we were about to part, he squirmed and said, "Madam, you see, I have got a new solution to the matter. Let me be sincere with you. If we eliminate him and we are caught, we shall say you sent us to eliminate him. They will hang us and give you a life sentence. To do it without the risk of investigations I suggest that, since you say he disturbs you at night, you go on an abrupt journey. Nobody around should know about it. We shall then waylay him by your house and when he comes and starts knocking, we shall pounce on him and shout thief, thief, thief. When the *quartier* hears the shouting, they will come out and beat the hell out of him and even roast him with tyres. Nobody will charge the *quartier* with murder. And that would be it. The chapter would be closed. No investigations, wonderful. How does that sound?" he asked briskly.

"It sounds wonderful – marvelously professional and very reassuring!" I exulted and added that it fell in line with my desire to go to Bamenda to see whether my parents had moved compound or not. I had sent word to the manager of the Rev. Sisters' bakery who was in charge of constructing the house for me to give my father the keys and ask them to move to the new compound immediately the doors were fitted. With that, I left for Bamenda the next day. I was in Bamenda for one week. When I returned my next door neighbour who perhaps had been eager to seize any opportunity to create acquaintance with me rushed in to tell me what happened in my absence.

"Madam," she addressed me with a series of handclapping and clucks and hums. "Welcome, welcome. God is with you. Welcome," she repeated and hissed to insinuate that something serious had happened or would have happened.

"Neighbour," I addressed her feigning surprise at her unconventional way of welcoming. "How, anything wrong?"

"Yes, I swear to God, you are lucky. Not only you, all of us in this *quartier*. They nearly burnt a thief alive in front of your house. I am telling you. A thief came to break into your house and two men with thick muscles like this," she demonstrated, "caught him and started shouting thief man, thief man. When the people heard and came to assist them, they started beating the thief mercilessly. Men, women and children came out with all types of weapons with which they beat him, not minding where. I have never seen even a snake beaten like that in my life. At a certain point, he collapsed on the ground. I thought he was dead. Some people then rushed to buy kerosene, some got tyres and piled them on him and others gathered papers and tried to set the tyres ablaze. Fortunately, because electricity has been very reliable these days, kerosene sellers did not replenish their stock – there was no kerosene in the *quartier*. The people who tried to light the tyres with papers and matches were disappointed because the flames from papers were not strong enough to set the tyres ablaze. That enabled the two muscular men to fence off the crowd and plead that the thief should not be burnt. If the man had been killed here, we all would have been looking for ways of doing traditional cleansing now; and you know how that costs. Thank God. Welcome."

"Thank you neighbour. I thank God that it did not happen. See, I am just a new person in this place. It would have been a terrible misfortune if they had killed the thief here. God is great. Thank you very much. I have just returned and I need some rest," I said and got up to indicate that she should go. She understood and when she went, I called the house-girl to find out what happened. She told me a thief was nearly killed in front of our house on the day I left for Bamenda. She added that the thief's life was saved by two muscular men who pleaded that he should not be killed.

"Did you see the thief?" I asked.

"No, we were hiding in the house when the people were trying to kill him," she responded.

"Did anybody look for me?" I asked.

"Yes. When the police came they asked where our parents were. I told them our dad had travelled long ago and that you had gone to see your sick mother in Bamanda that evening."

"What happened with the thief?" I asked.

"The police took him to the hospital," she responded.

"Did the police arrest any person?" I asked.

"No. They just asked the people to put the thief in their van and disperse. The van then went to the hospital.

With that, I knew the house-girl did not know that it was her uncle who was taken for a thief. For several days I waited for the thugs to come and make a report. Just when I was losing interest in it, the elderly one came. He smiled and wiped his brows.

"Welcome madam. The matter is closed. All went on well, very well as planned. That fellow is finished. He has to beg to eat. In the night of your departure, at about something past midnight, he came to your house pretty drunk and started knocking violently – a violent knocking that had all the ramifications of the intent to break the door. We pounced on him and disabled him by shattering the bones of his right hand. There is no way he can recover the use of his right hand. No magic can restore his hand. The fellow is finished. When he tried to resist with the left hand, we dislocated it at the wrist to spare him the loss of both hands. Then we started shouting thief, thief, thief to invite the *quartier* to come in for the real job. When the *quartier* heard the shouting they jumped out and started raining blows on him. He fell on the ground and seemed to have passed out. Some people fetched tyres and tried to set him ablaze. Fortunately the fire did not pick up. The people had wanted to finish with him before the police arrived. With the fire not picking up, my friend and I as if under the influence of astral forces, used our superior powers and skills to protect him from the angry crowd. Immediately the police van arrived we vanished from the scene. And that was it."

"Have you heard anything about him again? Where should he be now?" I asked.

"In a case like that, the police do a face-saving gesture by carrying the fellow to hospital and dumping him there at the mercy of the temperament of doctors and nurses. In most cases they hardly attend to thieves.

A thief that bad up may end up dying in hospital. Ever since thieves broke into the hospital and killed a medical doctor, they have been having it rough in our hospitals. Nobody attends to them."

"That is very unfortunate. Can you find out how he is doing and tell me later? I feel so bad about it now. I pray he should not die," I said and breathed in deeply.

"I can't dare go near him. Suppose he identifies me? Furthermore you had wanted him killed, now you want him alive – what a contradiction! If he had died there would have been a radio announcement calling his family to come for the corpse. I believe he is in bad shape but he will not die. We did not break his ribs and I did not see any mortal weapon used on his head. His chances of survival are fifty, fifty."

"Mr. Man, if you knew what led me to this, you would pity me. My body is still adamant but my soul is weak. Thank you. Is there any other thing?"

"No, you had paid us the 500,000 Frs. upfront."

"I thank you for avoiding bloodshed in this case. Take this 100,000 Frs. as compliment for saving me from the guilt of blood. Please, be upright and always go to church. Make sure you confess your sins." I said and handed him the money.

"Thank you madam. We are upright and we always go to church. As for what you call confession, we confess when we sin. In this case we have not sinned. We have simply done our job for money. We call that, filling the gap. To fill the gap means; to do mean jobs to fill the gap nature creates between the privileged and the disadvantaged. See, because my age and classmate's father was rich, he sent him to Lycee de Bonanjo, University of Yaounde, University of Paris 8, while I, fatherless, remained on the same spot. When he returned from Paris, he was appointed Treasurer General in Yaounde. In six months, he built a 100,000,000 Frs. mansion in the village. Though he was not of the royal family, he automatically became adviser to the *Chef* and was given all traditional titles. That was when this country was going through the worst political upheavals in its history. I got three mean jobs and was paid 150,000,000 Frs. for them. I also went and built a 100,000,000 Frs. more imposing house in the village. The two buildings are now proverbial showcases in the village and that makes both of us referential patriots. We have acquired all the titles and have been admitted into the *chef's* advisory council. I would not have had those honours 'until I sinned' but should I call it sin?

In this your case, we accepted 500,000 Frs. from you because first, you are a woman and second, because your man is not a bigwig. We don't accept anything less than 5,500,000 Frs. for a bigwig. You know why? It is because cases of bigwigs drag on and on with investigations sometimes instigated by international organizations at the request of the victim's family. When that happens we follow up with good cash and sometimes lose all what we got in the deal to seal leak-channels, what we call in professional jargon, springheads. Cases of simple folks don't last a day. The files are closed (if at all they were opened) immediately after burial. Who cares? We did your job well and in appreciation you have given us an additional 100,000 Frs. We thank you most heartily for that. But don't think 600,000 Frs. is a lot of money. It is not. It is just breakfast money for a few days and we go starving again. To be candid we can go for a year or two without a well-paying job," he said and stood up to go.

"I have heard but please, I am serious. Don't make a joke of it. Go to church and confess your sins," I advised.

"Madam, you tend to surprise me. What do you call sin? It is not a sin to carry out an assignment or pursue a course. When soldiers are asked to shoot and kill protesters, do they sin in carrying out the orders? No, the person who sins, if we should call it sin is the person who orders the shooting. In this case, if we had killed that your man, you would have been the sinner not us."

"But you told me that if you were caught, you would reveal that I sent you to kill him and they would hang you and give me a life sentence. That would be weighted justice – recognizing your dominant role in the crime," I explained.

"Yes madam. That is the ugly phase of the law. In reality, it should have been the other way round – that is, you for the gallows, and we for life; but those who enact laws and even those who execute them are not always aware of their full implications. Sometimes repressive governments get embarrassed when they send assassins to eliminate political opponents and the assassins are caught. In the past they hurriedly carried out the execution of the assassins to avoid the international press and Human Rights Groups investigations. Assassins soon realized their folly – instead of the **sender** being pursued, the **sent** was executed.

I once attended the International Assassins Conference (IAC) in Congo Brazzaville. After a heated debate, and basing their decision on the fact that the **sent** always became scapegoats, the attendees took the decision to halt the elimination of political opponents. Once political assassinations ceased, the opposition bounced back menacingly in most countries of the world and in some African countries, the opposition actually tookover power. That alarmed the hardcore repressive regimes and they raised the sum from 50,000,000 Frs. to 100,000,000 Frs. a single soul, payable upfront in a foreign bank of the **sent's** choice. The assassins scoffed at the bait and the governments had to take a new stand. Nowadays, when a government sponsored assassin is caught, the case drags on and on and ends in the assassin receiving a joyous life sentence," he explained.

"What do you mean by a joyous life sentence, can imprisonment ever be joyous?" I asked with a tint of anger.

"A joyous life sentence is a protracted imprisonment with life's desires on the platter of gold for both the prisoner and his family. In fact it is a decor of a life sentence. With time, it is reduced to no sentence at all by Presidential amnesties and in the end the prisoner walks out of the prison gates and is jetted into the full glow of world business. Or, as a better compensation he is made either an adviser to the President of the Republic, or a Roving Ambassador. Fantastic!" he responded excitedly.

"In spite of that, we should know what is right and what is wrong. Please, do as I have said," I pleaded and bid him farewell.

The rest of the matter was now between me and my loving Savior Jesus Christ. Was I right in taking revenge? Was the revenge proportionate? Was I actually divorced? What would be my stand in church – still a devoted choir mistress? Shall I remarry? Shall I remain without a child? First things first.

Chapter Sixteen

The most pressing thing to me was having a baby. Any other thing could wait. I was the lone child of my mother; and can you imagine how heartrending, how unalterably challenging and devastating the thought of the possibility of my ending up without a child was to us? In fact, the fear of being the full stop of my maternal linage stabbed us incessantly. I saw and pitied my stonehearted mother wither in agony. Her only hope of leaving a genealogy (the primary concern of my tribe) was gradually slipping away beyond recuperation. I believe it is a sin to surrender to the forces of misfortune. And so, I decided to put up a good fight whether married or not, to have my baby. Since I had just aborted, I thought I was still fertile. So, I decided to look for a baby before it was too late. The stakes were high. I had to be cautious and tactful to avoid another calamity.

I had imbibed 'Imeldametrix' and become a perfect blend. For my petals to be visited by only flying insects and not crawling ones, I dressed gorgeously, changed dresses four times a day, moved about with two pairs of shoes with high heels in the bag ready for use within a split second in sensitive places of convergence, did artificial overflowing long hair-transplant, wore make-believe eyelashes and nails, applied purple eye shadow, used expensive lipstick, and depending on the occasion, wore broad u-shaped-necked dresses and sprinkled my open bosom and back with microscopic shining flakes and finally laced all that with very expensive cologne. That was me – the product of Imelda's anvil, the newest Lady Bright.

The season of birthday parties in Bastos coincided with the arrival of the United Nations Diplomats sent to Cameroon to investigate allegations of marginalization and other discriminatory acts perpetrated against Anglophones. Some of the Diplomats attended the birthday party hosted by the Minister of Transport. While serving the cakes the Minister had asked me to make for the occasion, I put into full practice, 'Imeldaisms'. In addition to being strikingly dressed, I moved in short quick shuttling steps in high heels, swerved at 30 degrees to speak to the girls serving with me as they followed me from guest to guest, ran the tips of my left hand fingers across my forehead as if to train my hair, flicked my head time and again as if to frighten away flies trying to settle on my brows, and once in a while spoke some Americanisms to the girls. And lo and behold! Whenever I made a rearview of the attendees, I was amazed at what I saw. Most of the diplomats gazed up at me in rapture. I reciprocated with discrete, smart and tactful wiles – powerful eye-language. And as sure as daybreak, one picked up courage and reached out to me. He asked which modeling house I worked for. I said none, and asked why? He said because I was exquisitely marvelous in the art. I asked why? He stammered and lost train of thought, but recovered to propose I see him the next day at 5 o'clock in the evening at Hilton.

"What for?" I snapped in high pitch, feigning anger at the proposal.

"Just for a, a, an acquai acquaintance – a, a coke," he stammered in betraying loss of self-confidence.

"You guarantee my safety?" I asked, rolling my eyes enticingly to mend fences.

"Of course yes," he responded with revamped confidence.

"OK, I'll be there," I promised, flicked my head and left.

After the party, I reviewed the invitation in respect of my longing. It has to be a man of substance, not another gold prospecting fake. Yes. A personality in transit and therefore far removed from easy gossip. Yes. Known only to me. Yes. To seal the act and give credibility to the ploy of having no contest for the product. Yes. All correct. One hundred percent correct. Mission approved. *Embarquement immediat.*

The next day, I honoured the invitation and we established a hotline. And before long we found ourselves in a fantastic and agreeable union just after 'the folding of my Chinese flag'. By the time they left the country a month later, there were signals of my being double. A month later, I went and consulted the doctor who had diagnosed my first pregnancy and he confirmed. I asked him whether he would need assistance in following me up. He said I should enroll in his private clinic. I did, and he followed me up through the pregnancy.

When I was in the fourth month of pregnancy, I went to church to sanctify the pregnancy by confessing the sin(s) and receiving absolution. The Rev. Father saw me from a distance, recognized I was pregnant and being presumptuous of his forecast, with raised hands rushed to embrace me. He choked in the whirlwind of what to me was mistaken happiness and was seized by violent coughing. In half breaths, he stammered, "Emeren, E, E Emerencia, I told you, I told you, that that God is great. I see you pregnant. That is good. I told you that your husband would one day be a caring and loving one. Do you now believe what I said? Has it happened or not?" he asked.

"Please Father I have come for confession," I said, skipping what he expected.

"Yes, Emerencia. Let's, let's go to the church then," he suggested excitedly, and led the way. When we got to the confessional, he moved to the Rev's side and I moved to the sinner's side and knelt down.

"Please Father give me your blessings because I have sinned. It is one or two years if not more years, since I was caught up in a life-battle that made me forget whether I went to church on Sundays or not. Since then, I accuse myself of the following sins: I abrogated my marriage vow both in church and in court. I asked that my enemy be eliminated. He was instead maimed. I committed fornication and got pregnant. With these and those sins I cannot remember, I beg for your absolution."

It took the Rev. Father five good minutes to whisper, "Emerencia, you mean the child you are carrying is not that of your legitimate husband Pius?"

I whispered back, "Yes Father. I divorced Pius in your presence."

"Then you did not commit fornication. You committed adultery – a more serious sin. The church does not recognize your divorce."

"Father, who was married to Pius – the church or me? Who did he nearly kill – the church or me? Whose children did he kill – the church's or mine? Who then had the prerogative to divorce – the church or me? Please Father, pronounce your absolution and leave the rest to God."

"Emerencia, I can't do that right away. Let us retire to my office for a brief talk."

We retired to the Father's house and he sat me down for the talk.

"Emerencia, at the confessional, we do absolution of sins. But when there is an issue like yours that threatens the foundations of the church, we invite the concerned to our offices. I have invited you here to let you know that your views are contrary to church teachings and I would, considering the pillar you are in church, want you to change your mind. Pius your husband erred, but that does not warrant a breach of canon law. So I beseech you to change your stand. There is no sin God cannot forgive. Your sins shall be forgiven if you wholeheartedly repent and ask your eternal father to forgive you."

"Father, you think I am breaching canon law. I don't think so. Why can't you think that what God has put asunder man should not dare put together? In the beginning, God made man in his image and likeness and commissioned him/she to go and multiply. He did not say, go and sex for money or pleasure. He said, go and multiply. Sex must have a focus toward multiplication. Pius and I were in the process of multiplying. He knew that I was pregnant. He had had two children with other women; so he had fulfilled the obligation to a certain degree. Now when it came for him to make me fulfill my obligation, he, in his greed in thinking that he had had children and therefore children were not his priority, and despite the fact that I had opted to raise his children, consciously and in the most atrocious way murdered my twins. Am I not lucky to have survived that incident and its aftermath? Father, the canon law that approves of Pius' act is **unacceptable.** It is unacceptable Father. I say, it is unacceptable. It is not only unacceptable; it is inhuman and downright sordid and evil. It should not enter the annals of human thinking. It has no place in the world of human beings," I said and stood up to go.

"Please, Emerencia sit down. Now listen, canon law does not condone brutality. It simply protects the institution of marriage by upholding what our Lord and Savior Jesus Christ Himself had commended. And in doing that it relies on precautions taken before marriage. That is why we read the banns in sensitive places for a given period before we approve of the union. And once we are certain that all is well, we declare the couples married for better or for worse."

"Father, that is where lies the grave mistake. To stake canon law on what you call pre-marriage precautions is to exhibit ignorance of human nature. When I came here and you mistook my state for reconciliation with Pius, you told me that you had predicted that because Pius was human, he could change from bad to good. That was looking at only one side of the coin. Why didn't you think in being human, he could change from bad to worse, even worst? And if that happened it was incumbent upon the church to protect his victim? And if the church failed, as you have failed, the victim had the inalienable right to self-protection? I believe you are at it again. You are once again refusing to step out of illogicality, and doing the right thing. And by so doing, you are throwing the ball into my court. This places me in a helpless situation and in my helplessness therefore, I have no other option but to assume the powers to absolve my sins, especially those imposed on me by Pius' impiety,"

Immediately I said that, I was seized by a bout of trembling and profuse sweating - in the manner of an epileptic seizure. I thought I was drifting in an astral world, a world of celestial bliss. The Rev. Father apparently frightened by what he might have taken for demonic possession, withdrew from me and watched from a good distance as my physical body underwent the 'torture' of anointing. When the trembling stopped, and I regained my power of speech, I shouted, "Thank you Lord. Thank you Jesus. Thank you Holy Spirit," and in a loud voice made the pronouncement, **In the name of our Lord Jesus Christ who shed His holy blood to redeem the world from sin, I absolve myself and my expected child, of the sins forced on us by Pius. I command the power of the Holy Spirit to take possession of us that we may be accepted in the communion of saints. Amen.** When I finished, there was a rumble in my stomach. I breathed in deeply and moved out exhausted. While I moved away, the Father called out and asked, "Emerencia, are you all right?" I did not respond. I did not respond because in-between us, there was an inexplicable gorge. I moved on, confident in the rightness of what I had done and its effect on me and my child. Yes, I moved on. I remembered what our teacher once told us. He said that nothing good comes out of a status quo. A status quo must be challenged vigorously and only then can meaningful revolution spring out of it. Yes. And all meaningful revolutions have the temporary ugly phase. Yes. And their proponents hardly live long enough to see the work of their tender hands. Yes.

On Sunday, I went for communion. The Father hesitated in giving me communion. After Mass I attended the choir practice. In short, I reactivated all my church activities that a bad marriage had almost put to an end. My tummy was growing to the admiration of everybody. I had expected people to gossip about the father of my oncoming baby. But it seemed they were more interested in my being pregnant than in knowing who impregnated me. Or, it may be they did not know about the divorce. After all, even during the wedding, Pius' presence was inconsequential.

Imelda heard that I was pregnant and leading two other women friends came to visit me. Immediately they entered the house, there was a rumble in my womb. I rose and embraced them. Imelda brought all sorts of things – things her three children had not used and used. Because her in-law family was in London, whenever they heard that she was pregnant they simply flooded her with gifts of clothing and shoes for the baby. The other two women brought *koki corn* and palm oil respectively. I told them my odyssey and how I fought against the odds. I showed them my new acquisition and what I intended to do with the money that was coming in. Imelda praised me for my courage and said she was particularly happy that I was becoming a super star. After exhausting what we had to say, she stood up to return. I sent cakes to her children and promised to visit them, especially to ask her husband to help me buy a car.

"Brand new or secondhand?" she asked.

"Brand new." I responded.

"For a start, I prefer you buy a secondhand that will cost you three quarters less in price. After bashing it for one or two years (and that is of course unavoidable) you convert it into a taxi, school vehicle for the children or sell it and buy a prestigious new car to glorify your days on earth. I have always told you that life is meant for enjoyment not for unnecessary strain. The strain should be in childhood schooling and training to prepare for a better life. You are almost at the Zenith – husband or no husband."

"Thank you sister Imelda, you are always right," I said and we parted.

The other two women tallied for a while before they also returned.

Chapter Seventeen

My bitterness against Pius flamed on with no sign of its ever being reversed. Anything his, was evil and intolerable to me. But his children and the house-girl stuck on me like ticks. I did not want them to live with me and so create uncalled for acquaintances with my expected baby. I wanted to make my baby know that he/she was the only issue I had, if my next attempt happened to be futile because I had attained the end of my childbearing life. One morning I told my driver (I had bought a car) to drive the three children to Pius' house and abandon them there and tell them, "This is your father's house. If he cannot feed you, tell him to send you to your respective mothers." The driver did as I instructed but came to tell me that he met the door shut and the compound looked unattended to for a very long time. I said that was Pius' business. I entered the car and he drove me to school. When I returned from school, I met the children at Bonamoussadi in the bakery. They had been crying all day long. I went and told the Rev. Father that a situation that needed the interpretation of canon law had cropped up in my house – Pius' children had nowhere to live. I said I was afraid if they continued to live with me they could develop unnecessary attachments to me that would be detrimental to my expected child.

"Mrs. Pius," he addressed me.

"Former Mrs. Pius," I corrected.

"I'll still call you Mrs. Pius. I have not changed my stand on your issue."

"Then we can't talk Father," I responded and stood up to go.

"OK, Emerencia, sit down and listen to me. You once told me how in you magnanimity, you made your husband go for those children. I did not know that Pius was such an irresponsible person. The children now see you as their mother. Driving them away would be disastrous. So, accept to bear the inconveniences of bringing them up. God is going to grant you insurmountable mercies in your task of bringing them up. Please, let them be with you. Don't send them to Pius or their mothers."

"In that case, I have to protect my interests. There should be a document to show that I am not the mother of the children. The document should state unequivocally that the children are my foster-children and as such, have no claims to my property. This would be to secure the rights of my expected baby. I can't mince words here. Nobody knows when death would strike. If we establish that document and keep a copy here in the Mission and I take one home, I shall tell my friend Imelda about it and she would be able to defend the rights of my child if tomorrow, I am no more."

"Agreed. Dictate the terms."

"I have said the terms. Just prepare a document like that and sign as witness and look for somebody else to sign and I shall sign."

"Come tomorrow," the Father said and I returned. The next day he prepared a document stating clearly that my relationship with Pius' children did not warrant them to claim the right to inherit my property.

I was now counting days to deliver. Whenever my stomach rumbled, I called my driver to get ready to take me to the clinic. Several such skirmishes' kept me ill at ease. Then the time came to experience the glory of the woman. My under belly rumbled, I got into the car, within a minute, we were at the gate of the clinic, within a minute, I was in the labour room, and within another minute, my little boy-child screamed to acknowledge his arrival in the world. Tears of great joy flowed down my cheeks. The midwives and doctors, who were assigned to assist me because everybody expected a difficult delivery because of my late start in childbearing, were overjoyed. There, I, Emerencia, Lady Bright, Lady Bri, Sister Emeren, was a mother whether Pius liked it or not. I was a mother of a child beyond the reach of the assassin Pius.

The next day, the doctor discharged me saying there was no need for observation. I had had neither a tear nor any other anomaly to remain in the clinic.

When I got home with my little boy-child, Pius' children went mad with joy. Their emotional outpouring was unimaginable. They wanted to touch the child. They took turns to watch over him. They gave him all sorts of names. Pius' younger son in particular, opted to sleep with the child. I told him the cot was too small for the two of them. He then decided to sit by the cot and watch over him. After watching for a brief while, he succumbed to sleep and the house-girl took him to their bed. In the morning he refused to go to school because he wanted to watch over the child. To lure him to go to school, I asked the driver to take them to school for the first time in my car. He still refused going to school. I insisted he should go to school and promised he would hold the child immediately they returned from school. He accepted and as they entered the car, he pinned his face on the back windscreen to see truly that he was being taken away from the child. When they returned, he refused to eat until I made him hold the child. So, I sat him down and helped him hold the child for a couple of minutes. When I withdrew the child from him he was full of joy. He ate and fell asleep. It was a wonderful manifestation of... what should I call it – love, devotion or excitement?

Guilt tore through my heart when I remembered what I had forced the Rev. Father to write against the children. I saw how one man's sin had sewn desolation among us. I took quick action to make good the emotional outpouring. I went to the Rev. Father with my copy of the document and told him to tear up the document. He asked why, I told him about the magnanimity of the children and why I had changed my mind on them. I said I had decided to regard all of them as my children and give them equal opportunities in life. I said I had the means, and would give all of them the best education and whoever proved to be a leader, would be made to lead his brothers. The Father was amazed. He moved towards me and whispered, "Emerencia, you are marvelous." Then he got the document and using his cigarette lighter, burnt it and put the ash in a little tube and gave me to take home.

"Father, why should I take this home? I don't want anything to remind me of my guilt."

"That is the more reason why you must take it home and keep it where you can see it every minute to remind you even in the most difficult times that you have sworn to be the mother of all the children. Bringing up children is very tempting. Children are unpredictable. A good child may turn out bad the next minute for no apparent reason. So, don't waver. You have taken a good decision. Thank you, God bless you."

I returned from the Mission relieved of my tension. I put the tube by the side of the cot. The next day, I told the driver to take the children for vaccination to immunize them against school diseases.

Chapter Eighteen

If I had lost twins, I was now a mother of triplets. Pius' children behaved as if they were remote-controlled. Wherever the baby lay, they were there. If neighbours came to 'hold' the baby as it is customary with us, one of them would stand by her right and place his hand on her shoulder and the other would stand by her left and place his hand on her shoulder. They would do the same from lady to lady. They gave the baby the name Cuckoo. What it meant, I don't know. If somebody asked them, "Who is your father? They would respond, "I don't know." If somebody asked them, "Who is your mother?" They would respond, "The mother of Cuckoo." Though that was pretty tantalizing, it gave me some sort of mystical aura. If we called the first boy by his name David, he would not answer. Same with his junior brother, Peter. They both preferred to be known as brother of Cuckoo. So to differentiate them, the first was called Cuckoo 1, the second, Cuckoo 2 and my son, Cuckoo 3. I shortened the Cuckoo to Cucks – Cucks I, Cucks 2 and Cucks 3. They in return called me *momi* Cuckoo. And so we lived in our Cuckoo family

One day, I received a letter by post from my son's father in New York saying they were coming to Cameroon again for a three week mission to find out the true political situation of Southern Cameroons before independence and reunification. He said he would be in Hilton, same room. I nearly fainted. I knew I had told nobody about the father of my child. I knew I had not even informed him that he had left me pregnant in the first encounter. Was his coming a pretext to claim the child? Should I surrender the child to him if he asked for him? What should I do to thwart his attempt of taking my child away? I read the letter several times and concluded that he did not know that I had his child. The ploy had worked.

I was in the eleventh month of nursing my child and had just gone through my flowering. Although I had wanted to breastfeed him for at least a year some months before venturing into looking for another, the temptation was great. And once his father came, we consummated. He never asked me about my child and so I knew he did not know that he had a son with me. For two weeks, I belonged to him. At the end of the mission when he was preparing to leave, he asked me what I thought he could do for me. I shrugged my shoulders.

"OK, I will have you employed by the UN and sent to Abidjan, Ivory Coast. You like that?"

"No," I responded. "I can't leave one African country for another."

"Then you'll work with Care Cameroon," he promised.

That evening, I invited him to have dinner with me in a Chinese Restaurant in Bastos. I told him he could come along with two friends. Perhaps taking me for one of those street girls tourists picked by the walls of hotels, he was bemused at the thought of me shouldering dinner for four people in a Chinese Restaurant. He estimated 300, 000 Frs. for food and drinks, mostly wine.

"Emerencia, I am sorry, I can't help you in paying the bill. I have only my travelers' cheques for any eventuality now with me. Would you mind taking me alone to a cheaper restaurant?" he asked.

"I did not say you would help me pay the bill. I have invited you and any two friends. If you don't have friends we shall go, two of us," I responded.

"OK. When do you come for us? Will you like the use of our diplomatic vehicle?"

"No. I have a vehicle – a brand new Mercedes 300."

"At 7.00 p.m., I took the father of my son and two of his friends to the China Town Restaurant and after eating and wining I was given a bill of 285,000 Frs. I took out of my handbag a Standard Chartered Bank Cheque Book and wrote out a cheque and handed it to the restaurant assistant. He took the cheque without hesitation to the surprise of my guests who said they had witnessed the refusal of cheques of other banks by restaurant managements in Bastos. At 10.00 p.m. we returned to the hotel and I bid them goodbye. They were to take off at midnight.

I returned to my house with a throbbing heart. Would things work miraculously again? O Lord! That they did, according to your will. Then I started singing my song 'Serving the living God'. I sang it. I hummed it. I cooed it. Yes, I was serving the living God. Sleep intervened and the peace of the Lord enveloped me.

About 80 days after the departure of my son's father, I started having nausea – spiting a lot of saliva. A woman's body is a complex machine and one can't say with certainty that alike signs would produce similar results. So, I went and consulted my doctor. He gave me a series of tests to carry out. The results confirmed my speculations. I was pregnant. I went to Briqueterie and bought the most expensive laces and sewed overflowing gowns to camouflage my pregnancy. An elephant can do all other things but it cannot hide. By the fourth month, the pregnancy could be hidden no more. I carried my head high and did all my things with no complexes. I was Lady Bright forever. As usual, people tended to appreciate my being pregnant than gossiping about who was responsible. First, nobody around Bonamoussadi and its peripheries had intimately seen my pants apart from perhaps seeing them on the drying line. Second, the extremes of my life; that is, the contrast between the one-gown-day-and-night-working Emerencia and the sophisticated-Imelda-forged Emerencia, Lady Bright, had a tantalizing effect on the people of Bonamoussadi vis-à-vis their relation with me. To put it simply, when I was down, nobody looked at me. When I rose, I was too sophisticated for people of Bonamoussadi to dream of coming near. Thus my prestige was upheld all over. Well, for the Rev. Father, there was a gap between his reasoning and mine.

Chapter Nineteen

Six months into my pregnancy, I received a letter of employment from Care Cameroon, employing me as Assistant Director in charge of Refugee Affairs in Cameroon – a post that had been the reserve of men since its creation but which most of them, especially the one I was replacing had disgracefully abused. I went and saw the Director General of Care Cameroon and told him my problem. I was pregnant and so I could not take up duties until I delivered. If Care could not wait, they could look for somebody else. The Director was stunned by my frankness. That was a post high government officials, mostly Ministers, scampered for, for their relatives, but here was a person who would sacrifice it on principles.

"Madam, I think you can take up duty as from tomorrow just to acquaint yourself with its demands. You are entitled to a three months paid maternity leave that can be spread on demand – one month before you deliver and two months after you deliver or vice versa," he said.

"That would be very OK with me. Thank you very much," I responded and after a brief chatting on other things, I left to prepare to start work the next day.

The next day I was installed as Assistant Director for Refugees Affairs in Cameroon, in a small but dignified ceremony. I was taken round the premises to see the offices under my jurisdiction. Wherever I went the junior staff tended to be extremely happy. I shook hands with them and chatted with those I could chat with. There was a little reception at the end of the tour of the place and after that I returned home to my Cuckoo children.

The next morning I was at my job site at 7.30 a.m. The junior staff was all there. The sweepers had swept the offices in the evening and only came that early to dust the tables. Work started immediately. I asked for the files of protest letters and complaints. Then I got the files of conditions of employment. I browsed through them, took notes, then asked for the files describing the requirements of my work and browsed through them and took notes. By closing time I had gone through the files describing the protocol of Care. The next day, I did not treat files. I went from one office to another interviewing the workers on what pleased and displeased them in Care Cameroon. The cry was the same – the former Assistant Director and his predecessors had eaten 'theirs and theirs'. That was a common disease in Cameroon where those in power ate their much, plus the little of the downtrodden. After listening to the junior staff I interviewed the senior staff. In four days of interview, I was confident I would offer my best services to Care Cameroon.

I was placed on a salary six times greater than what I earned as a teacher. I had a service Pajero with a driver. I had free housing in Bastos – free water and electricity. I was in charge of the construction of makeshift housing in nearby war zones, and Tchad was a war zone. I was in charge of food distribution to refugees. I was in charge of the education of the children of refugees. In short, my job was so lucrative that working there for one year only, a greedy person would become a multimillionaire. With that bag of knowledge, I waited when, after delivery I would take up duty fully to implement what I thought would be good for Care Cameroon.

The months rolled by and I gave birth to another boy – my 4th Cuckoo boy. David was gradually outgrowing the Cuckoo syndrome and so did not show much enthusiasm when I brought in my second child. But Peter was as usual, mad with joy. He liked the aloofness of David. The 3rd Cucks was too young to show any concern. My fears that my early pregnancy would retard his growth and robustness were unfounded. He was unperturbed, smart and agile. He had perfected his walking by the time his junior brother came and could play with Cucks 2 with ease. I spent most of my two months pre-delivery maternity leave with them at Bonamoussadi, while my Bastos house was being renovated.

I moved to Bastos two weeks after the completion of the renovation. My compound was fenced and protected with powerful electronic gadgets. I had three cars – my first car that took the children to school, my brand new Mercedes, and the Pajero. Before I left Bonamoussadi, I asked the manageress of the bakery to move to my abode and so create more space for the expansion of the bakery. Since my house in Bastos was furnished I left her with my furniture. She was now fully in charge of the bakery and the Real Estate businesses. I raised her salary from 80,000 Frs. to 130, 000 Frs. but gave her only 80,000 Frs. after all she was living in a free house. So she knew she was saving 50, 000 Frs. every month.

When I resumed work fully after delivering, I was paid 12,000,000 Frs. for three months salary and maternity leave allowance. I took six million and bought a six thousand square metre piece of land at Nkolmesen and had it fenced. I divided it into two – 5000 square metres for myself, and 1000 square metres for the manageress of the bakery. When her savings covered the price of the 1000 square metres, I went and showed her, the land. She went mad with joy.

At the job place, I reinstated all the allowances my predecessors had deprived the junior staff. I instituted compensation for productivity, honesty and respect for hierarchy. The harder the person worked the more money they got. The more honestly a worker presented his/her problem the better attention it received and the more a worker respected the hierarchy the more chances they had for favours. I raised risk allowances especially for workers at war zones.

Within three months, the Director of Care Cameroon called me to congratulate me for the new spirit I was inculcating in the workers. He was receiving fewer complaints, work was improving, gossips were dying down, workers were becoming more enthusiastic and the refugees for whom we worked were receiving what belonged to them. Although we had not had a major crisis, there were signs that we would handle one efficiently when it came. At the end of the year, I was given a medal for organizational ability.

I held a party in my house to celebrate the medal. My Cuckoo children, to my surprise had prepared a song for me and asked me to allow them sing it to the invitees. I begged the indulgence of the invitees and gave them the floor. David and the house-girl holding Cucks 4, stood behind, and Cucks 2 and Chucks 3 stood in front facing the audience. Then the house-girl intoned the song – **Our mama is great**, "one, two, three, sing.

> Our mama is great,
> Our mama is kind
> Our mama is just
> Our mama feeds the poor.
> Our mama is blessed
> Our mama has us four
> Our mama feeds us well

Our mama is Lady Bri.
Our mama we love you
Our mama God loves you
Our mama Care loves you
Our mama is blessed.

The applause that followed was deafening. Throughout my life, I had never been subjected to that type of emotional outpouring. My faced twitched in a series of suppressed hiccoughs as tears of great joy built up in my eyes. I took my kerchief and covered my face and in the blur of things, I saw other invitees wiping tears from their eyes. The Director of Care Cameroon led the way. He pulled out 100,000 Frs. and slammed it on the face of the house-girl. Other dignitaries followed with varied amounts. The representative of the refugees gave them 5000 Frs. It was marvelous. At the end of the day, the children had 630,000 Frs.

When the singing was over they came coddling around me and I petted them in the most affectionate manner. I was so proud. I need not say that the party was a great success. In acknowledging its success, the representative of the refugees said if they were to have administrators like me, they would never want the war to end for them to return home. He praised my administration for having a human face and prayed that God should prolong my stay on earth. The representative of the junior staff said that for the first time in his working life he went home straight from work to meet his wife and children instead of going to the bar to dispel his frustrations at work. Then the Director General of Care concluded that on the first day he met me and I thought of turning down the appointment because I was indisposed to execute it, he knew, he had at last found the person who would handle the job well. He congratulated me and added that he would be going on retirement very soon and I should be ready to take up greater responsibilities. What that meant, I did not know.

At the end of the party I called the children, showed them the money and asked them what they wanted to do with it. Cucks 2 wanted it used in buying sweets. Cucks 1 wanted a ball. The house-girl did not know what to do with it. I suggested we give 200,000 Frs. to the church for a special Mass, use 200, 000 Frs. to buy the uniform we shall wear during the mass and the rest of the money throw a party for the people who will attend the Mass. "Yaaaa," they approved.

After that, I slumped into my sofa to count my blessings and woes one by one. I had bought a piece of land in a strategic place for my Cucks children, which when shared would give each of them at least 1000 square metres. In the same vein, I had enabled the faithful manageress of my bakery to procure a plot in the same place. I was saving 15,000 Frs. every month for the house-girl to help her learn a trade by the time she left me. I had a bakery and Real Estate businesses that earned for my children, hard cash. I had moved my parents from the Stone Age environment to the city-centre where they had a self-contained house. I had successfully banished Pius from me and was giving his children the best amenities available. I was Assistant Director of an international organization. All the workers approved of my relation with them. I had three vehicles, my first car which now carried my children to school, my brand new Mercedes in which I took my children's father for dinner, and my official Pajero which I used for field work. I was living in a house and compound in which if death were a thunderstorm, it won't see me. I had written a project awaiting the signature of the DG, putting the six 70 year old night watchmen my predecessor had on record that they had a monthly wage of 60,000 Frs. but whom in reality he paid only 30,000 Frs. a month. They would be pensioned on a lump sum of 5,000,000 Frs. each. And above all, I was as devoted to my Lord and Savior as ever before. The children and I had offered the Mass and thrown the party as we had agreed to do. My popularity was growing by leaps and bounds and there were no occasions in Yaounde to which I was not invited. I believe I am not bragging, so, judge me Lord.

I cannot however say that all that glitters is gold. No, I can't. My fortunes or misfortunes with Pius are like an abscess in my armpit. And whether I like it or not, whenever an interested person asks me why I am carrying up my arm, I must say, because I have an abscess in my armpit. Yes, as simple as that. I did hear that Pius was given good treatment in hospital because he was lucky that, just before his incident, the Human Rights Commission had protested against the non-treatment of wounded thieves in Yaounde and Douala hospitals; and the Minister of Health had responded by giving stern warnings against any such unethical revenge. According to my informant, Pius responded very well to the treatment and was later taken to Oku for traditional treatment of his broken bones. There were possibilities of his partial or full recovery and I prayed for it. But I wonder whether I regret what happened and how it happened.

Pius' abscess in my armpit is also realized in his child Cucks 2, whose mother is still alive. I don't know how that child will feel if one day he happens to meet his real mother. Will he say that because blood is thicker than water, he would have been better off if he had been brought up by his real mother? I wonder how his mother will feel if she happens to know that her child looked onto another woman as his mother. Will she react by assailing me and demanding that I give back her son, my Cucks 2? I am asking for advice, even from you. Should I look for her and tell her the truth about her child? Should I tell my Cucks boy, I am not his real mother? And how far should I go to convince the Rev. Father that it is she who wears shoes that pinch who should determine where, when and how to remove them and not the cobbler?

Sincerely yours,
Lady Bright.